AS BRIGHT AS THE STARS

CINDY NICHOLS

egan Lewis pulled her coat around her and tightened her scarf as the cold sliced through her on her way back to the stables. This was not at all how she'd thought it would be. When her sister had come to her with the idea of opening a residential rehabilitation home for challenged teenage girls, she'd hoped it would be a wonderful way to finish up her career in education. She'd worked with tough kids before, back in California, but the thought of lending her experience and expertise to needy kids in Arizona—and the idea of working with her sister—had won out. After several years, she'd begun to question how much they were helping and whether they had the stamina—and money—to do a good job of it.

Her hand tightened around the phone in her pocket and her heart was still warm from the conversation she'd just had with her daughter, Cassie. The news that the vaquita sanctuary would be working out after all and was already in progress was a dream come true for her daughter—and it had been really difficult to tell Cassie that she couldn't visit in the foreseeable future. Too much to do at the girls' home.

Her call had been interrupted by a message from one of the staff members that Emily, an especially troubled and volatile kid who had been at the house for a while, had left class and headed toward the stables. Megan peered across the field and spotted Emily, quickening her pace.

Head down, she followed the teenager with the baseball bat toward the stables. "Emily, I can't let you do this. You know I can't," she said, her voice edged with fatigue.

"I'm sick of this place, and I'm leaving," the girl said, her black hair billowing around her face. The bat had been at her side when she stormed from the kitchen of the group home. Now, she gripped it with both hands and raised it over her head. "Emily, we've been talking about this for months. You do these things, then you change your mind and want to stay. What about Tigger? That horse loves you." Megan inched toward the furious girl, hoping this would be the time Emily came around, choose not to be violent. She could always hope. As director of the group home, hope was essential.

Turning to look at Megan, Emily's arms trembled as the bat crashed down on the door of the barn, splinters flying in the evening sun. The bat sailed through the air, thudding into the wall of the stable that housed Tigger, the horse Emily had been caring for during for the past few months of her stay at the ranch. Horse therapy hadn't been helpful for this one.

"Emily? I thought you loved Tigger," Megan said to Emily's back as the teenager ran into the stable, pulling the door behind her.

"What was that about?" Megan heard her sister and business partner Annie ask as she rushed up behind her. "What set her off this time?"

"Heck if I know. They were in class, and one of the girls called her on something she didn't like. She just went off. Grabbed the bat and ran out here."

"I called 911. Megan, we can't do this with her anymore. We're both losing sleep over her, and the other girls are scared. She's got to go."

Megan stared at the closed stable door. "It's so hard to give up on her. But I've completely gone through my bag of tricks, and she just can't keep it together. I know you have, too."

Even in Arizona, the high desert got snow, the wind biting through her clothes. "I'll call her case worker and make arrangements for her to leave. It's just so sad. I hate to give up on her."

"I know, but we've done good work here. We can't save all of them, and she needs more help than we can give. We'll make sure she finds it."

Dust plumed from the desert road, the red lights of

the sheriff's car flashing. "Well, we definitely can't save this one," Annie said. "She's still better than when she came, so I'll take that for comfort."

"I guess it's all relative, but yes, she actually is better. I'd forgotten she was much worse when she arrived. We really have helped her."

Annie nodded slowly. "I'll stay here with Emily. You can take the sheriff this time." She smiled, motioning toward the flashing lights. "I'm sure you've had enough of this by now."

Megan wearily explained to the sheriff what was going on, and he nodded in understanding. He'd made several trips out to the ranch for girls that needed more than they could provide at the ranch, and he'd become a sympathetic and supportive ally over the years.

"I got this, Megan. And don't feel bad. It happens sometimes. She'll find the help she needs, but we can't have her scaring the other girls."

Megan leaned against the sheriff's car and rested as she watched the sheriff and Annie deftly convince the angry teenager that calming down a bit and going with the sheriff was in her—and everyone else's—best interest. It was usually a job Megan did herself as she had lots of experience at calming people down, but she was grateful that this time it hadn't fallen to her. She was weary and she knew it.

Emily hadn't quite given up the fight. The sheriff guided Emily to the car in handcuffs as she hurled expletives at the wide-eyed girls watching from the second-story porch. "What are you looking at?" she yelled, spitting in the dirt.

As the girls were shepherded back into the house by the staff she and her sister had carefully selected and trained, Annie threw her arm around Megan's shoulder. "Look, Megan, it's been a rough couple of months. Why don't you take some time off and head to Playa Luna? Swim in the ocean. Walk on the beach. See your daughter. Plan a wedding. Daniel and I can handle this for a while," she said, her eyes filled with concern.

"I can't leave you here alone with this," Megan said, shaking her head. "We started this together. I can't leave now."

"Look, with Emily gone for more specialized treatment, the other girls will be a piece of cake. No worries. Just take a couple of weeks off. See if Felicia can meet you there. And you know Cassie's been dying to have you come. She even called me to ask when that might be."

Megan's thought of her daughter, Cassie. Whenever she did, she almost burst with pride—Cassie had not only pulled off creating the sanctuary for the endangered vaquita, but was engaged to the love of her life and living on the Sea of Cortez, fulfilling her dreams.

"I'll see if Felicia can meet me. Are you sure? I feel like this is a lot to leave you with."

"Like I said, now's a good time. Leave tomorrow."

Megan smiled at her sister. "I do think I could use a break."

"Good. So, now that you've agreed to go, I need to let you know something. You can use the time to think about some things."

"Uh-oh. I usually get bad news first." She rubbed her eyes as she waited for the next bomb to drop.

"I just got an email that the state's cut funding again for teen rehab. At this level of funding, we'll be lucky if we can just pare down to a mac and cheese program," Annie said, exhaustion seeping into her voice, too. "We've given up everything for this ranch. We won't even be making enough money to feed the girls well, let alone the horses. And when we quit our jobs to do this, we agreed to make this the best program in the state. We said we would never do a mac and cheese level program."

The last two years had taken a toll on her, too, and she looked defeated, her shoulders sagging.

"And, when you're in Mexico, think about the bigger question. Are we really happy?"

Megan hugged her sister and they both turned toward the house as the sheriff's car disappeared out of sight.

Her head spinning from the day's events and the new information, Megan took her time on the short walk back to the little house she had called home since she moved from California. For three years, the group home they'd dreamed of creating had struggled financially, no matter what they tried.

The horses were quiet as the cold wind whipped

through the stables, and her riding boots kept her warm as she padded through the mud. The garden she had planted when she'd arrived had completed its harvest, its zucchini and tomatoes dormant as the leaves turned golden. Passing through the garden she had grown, she looked toward the fountain in the middle, and the tree that had doubled in size since she had planted it last summer. Its leaves were dropping as fall set in, the bitter wind a daily occurrence now. A hummingbird buzzed at one of the lavender plants, darting off toward the wilting flowers. The dream of a new life and new business was fading along with the garden.

With a sigh, she dialed the number of her oldest friend, Felicia. As the phone rang, she thought of the last time she'd seen her—when Alex had flown them out to surprise Cassie at the groundbreaking cere-monies for the vaquita sanctuary and the new resort they'd be building near the south campos. Everyone had been concerned the resort in its original design would cause much damage to the small fishing community, and Megan and Felicia had been thrilled that the resort plans had changed into more of an eco-friendly destination with kayaking rather than golf. Well, everybody but her golf-crazy friend, Felicia.

"Hey, Flee, want to take a trip to Playa Luna?" she said into the phone as her friend answered. "I've got some time off and I'm heading down. Come with me."

"What? You can get away? Gosh, you know I'd love

to, even though I'd been hoping to golf down there with the new resort."

Megan rolled her eyes, checking that comment off the list of phrases she knew she'd be hearing.

"I've been working too much myself. Kyle has a break from his residency and wants to head down to talk to the doctor in town about volunteering and do some fishing, anyway, so great timing. I'm in."

"Can you leave as early as tomorrow?" Hope swelled her heart as it seemed it might be possible to be at the beach this time tomorrow.

"It works for me. Just got off a long run of vet shows, so I'm good. See you at the usual place. Does noon work?"

Megan's heart lifted a bit and she felt a smile spread across her face. "I'll just pack a few things and we can shop there. See you then." She hung up and did a little twirl in her tiny kitchen. Tomorrow might just be a better day after all.

CHAPTER 2

*A*fter a quick goodbye to Annie, Megan hopped in her car and started the drive to the town on the border of California and Arizona where she and Felicia had agreed to meet. She'd spent some time thinking, enjoying the solitude, and when it wasn't too early—she'd left at dawn—she called Cassie. Her daughter didn't normally like surprises, but Megan figured that since Cassie had been calling and asking her to come, this surprise would be welcome. She wasn't disappointed.

"Mom, that's fantastic," Cassie cried when Megan told her the news. "I even called Aunt Annie and asked when you could get away. Alex and I are ready to set a date and I need some help."

"Oh, Cassie, it's perfect. I'm so excited for you," Megan said, and she was. They caught up as the miles flew by, and Cassie insisted that she and Alex come by the house later in the evening for a hug and hello. Megan ended the call with her heart full, not believing her good fortune that in several hours she'd not only be in her beautiful brick house by the sea, listening to the sound of the waves, but she'd be with Cassie. It was almost too good to be true.

She called Felicia, who was coming from the opposite direction, and they talked through a grocery list. Right at noon, they met in the Walmart parking lot, the last store they'd see before the crossed the border. It was their usual spot—they'd been meeting there for years. Megan gave her friend a hug and was happy to do the same with Felicia's son, Kyle, and she got some extra kisses from Russell, Felicia's Jack Russell Terrier who came everywhere with her. She still marveled at the six-foot tall, handsome man Kyle had become and she loved seeing his wide, warm smile. She hadn't seen him often lately as he'd had his head down in medical school and his residency, so seeing him in shorts and flip-flops, his baseball cap askew, made her happy.

Breezing through the grocery section, they bought the same things they'd been getting for years in anticipation of their trips. They'd been doing this for twenty-five years, and had it down. Wine, chips and cheese for nachos, jalapenos, steaks. "Don't forget the margarita mix and tequila," Felicia called from the tortilla aisle.

"Got it," Megan said, wheeling the cart back to the

alcohol aisle. If she was to forget her troubles at the ranch, this was a good aisle to be in.

They threw the groceries quickly in the car, packing the ice chest with things that needed to stay cold and high-fived each other as Kyle secured everything as they got ready to cross the border. It felt good to be taking a road trip.

"If Taylor and Cassie were here, we'd need to be getting Slim Jim's," Megan said with a laugh.

"Do you think they still eat those things?" Felicia said. Their daughters had started a tradition of really bad road trip food that they discouraged them from eating any other time. Road trips, yes. Real life, no.

"I sure hope not, but I bet they would on a road trip. They've been taught well." She smiled at the memory of bringing the girls down, and the fun they'd had with the exception of a few minor scrapes involving quads and mud.

Felicia hopped in the car with Megan, Kyle following in their Excursion.

"The truck's full of new patio furniture and new rugs and tons of cool stuff for the house. I can't wait to get down and see how things look." Her beach neighbor always brought something new. "So what's happening at the ranch?" Felicia asked as they settled in for the rest of the drive.

"I don't even know where to start," Megan said. "It's so awful, it's almost funny." Gripping the steering wheel tighter, she shared the events of the day before.

"I don't know how you do it. I'd have to smack those girls. You're a saint."

Megan laughed, knowing Felicia wouldn't smack anybody even if she had the chance. "I'm not a saint. Just trying to hold onto the business at this point, and do as much good as we can."

"You said your funding got cut. How bad is it?"

"Worse than bad. Something's got to change."

"Well, I always thought you were crazy for taking that chance," Felicia said with a smile. "Especially at our age. This close to retirement is no time to be taking a risk like that."

"Gee, thanks."

"You know what I mean. Taking out all of your retirement and moving to another state? What were you thinking?"

Megan paused for a moment, running the whole decision-making process through her head for the thousandth time. "I believed that it would be a rewarding job and financially stable, or I wouldn't have done it. I'm not that much of an idiot," she said, rolling her eyes at her friend. "And you know I've spent my entire career trying to help people who started out behind the gate."

"I know. Who could have predicted the budget cuts? Not an ideal time to start a new business.

"That's an understatement," she said, trying to find some humor in the situation.

"I guess the timing was just awful," she said, as they

pulled into the Mexican fishing village of San Felipe, the Sea of Cortez shining on the horizon. "You know, my whole life, I got every job I ever applied for. It never really occurred to me that this might fail. Guess that is actually the definition of an idiot," she said, laughing.

She had sincerely believed, in the beginning, that things would go easily and the new business would be a booming success. Who wouldn't want to send their troubled girls to a beautiful horse ranch, allowing them to heal from their trauma? Enter the state-wide cuts, wiping out public funds like a tsunami. And her personal funds, as well. Daniel and Annie had done the same, and the business was on its last financial legs, no nest eggs left to infuse cash into the ranch. Sheer determination to help the girls had kept them in business longer than they should have been. Now things were dire, and the worry lines creeping onto her face were permanent.

Determined not to think about it for a while, she slowed down to pass through the last fishing village before the south campos. She couldn't believe she was heading down to her favorite spot on earth, Playa Luna. She'd bought the beach house there when she had had some money, never thinking it might become all she had left.

Her sour mood lifted as they drove through the town, the streets lined with vendors hawking their colorful wares. Mexican fishing boats, pandas, dotted the beach, their owners hawking rides for the day and promising a great catch. The famous blue San Felipe shrimp were available everywhere, in iced bins along the malecon and eager tourists lined up to buy them by the kilo, anxious to sample some local treats.

"Want to do any shopping?" Felicia asked with a grin.

Megan shook her head and laughed. "You know as well as I do we've bought one of everything around here over the years. I don't need another blanket or sombrero. Let's just get there."

The graceful rhythm of the sea calmed her even more as they headed further south, falling into a comfortable silence. The road wound close to the shore and then back toward the desert again for the remaining twenty-mile stretch to their little community, Playa Luna. Here, in the south campos, the houses dotted the shoreline with their solar panels flashing. The all-solar community consisted of all types of houses, from grand adobe houses to trailers with a cover, and all kinds in between.

"I can't wait to see how the house is holding up. So glad we finished it last year, and glad to be out of the trailer," Felicia said, gazing down the long dirt road toward camp. "And you—you've got all new solar panels and electricity. I know where I'll be heading if mine goes out. That sure was great of the girls and Alex to get that fixed for you."

"It sure was, but I don't think they had a choice. It was that or flashlights, but it really worked out great.

We were only here for a couple days for the resort ground-breaking that I really didn't get to test it."

"Well, we'll have a chance now."

"We will," Megan said as she pulled into Playa Luna and just being this close to the sea had her breathing easier already. "Cassie and Alex are coming over tonight, so I can thank them again."

"Great," Felicia said as she rolled down her window and stuck her head out, the wind blowing her short, blonde hair all around. "I can make my world famous nachos for them."

Megan laughed—Felicia's nachos weren't world famous but they were pretty much the only thing her friend knew how to make, and she would be grateful to have them.

They pulled into camp and savored the sights and smells. As they pulled up to the yellow house that Felicia and her kids had started the prior year, Megan glanced to the other side of the dirt road, the pull strong.

"You and Kyle okay here?" she asked, as they stretched after the long drive.

"No problem. I've got help." She pointed at Kyle and gestured across the road. "Go on and head over. Holler if you need anything. Kyle and I will unload. I'll be over in an hour or so."

She was happy to see her ladrillo brick house across the road intact, inviting her to stay and rest for a while.

CHAPTER 3

egan gazed down the dune and over to Sea of Cortez, the sparkling water inviting. As she headed through the sand, her memory suddenly got the best of her, and she shook her head with worry, wondering how she'd ever sort things out with the business. Memories of the girls' ranch slipped in, and the familiar knot of anxiety gripped her stomach. It had been more constant than not the last few years, and she hoped some time in her most cherished place would ease it a bit, and bring some clarity.

Lost in her thoughts, she crossed the road between the houses, anxious to stand on the bluff and breathe in the soft ocean air. If anything could clear the cobwebs out of her head and maybe leave enough room for solutions to come in, it would be the view from the cliff.

She jingled the keychain with the fish bottle opener

on it, the key to the house painted with daisies. She'd picked out that key especially when she had new ones made for her beach house purchase. Daisies, and a leopard print for the garage. Her smile grew as she remembered the happy times she'd spent here. It was the one place where she felt she could even try to be carefree. Happy. That's all she wanted to be. Happy.

The cool ocean breeze whipped through the open doors facing the cliff. Pulling back the curtains, the serenity of the house enveloped her. *Peaceful*, she thought, the sun shining into the house, casting light on the beautiful ladrillo bricks the house was built with.

I've been away far too long, she thought, giving her house a good once-over. The blue marble of the bath reflected the incoming sunlight, warm and inviting. She cherished time with lots of friends, but the trip down for the ground-breaking had been quick. She hadn't had time alone, and she was looking forward to some of that. "We have a date tonight, you and I," she said, running her hands over the cool stone. Opening the drawer under the ceramic floral sink, she pulled out candles and bubble bath, setting them on the counter for later. Stepping out onto the arch-covered patio, she inhaled the cool sea breeze, the air not quite reaching her soul.

Her heart and body begged her to rest, but she had work to do. Houses off the grid were a little bit more work than others, but the routine of opening up the house was familiar, and she knew it like the back of her hand. She flipped on the water pump, turned the spigot on the propane tanks and quickly lit the water heater and refrigerator. She looked around, confident she wasn't missing anything, and unloaded the car. It didn't take long as she hadn't brought much, and since Felicia wouldn't be over for a bit longer, she took her time and unpacked her clothes, thinking how nice it felt to be staying for a chunk of time.

She gave the counters a wipe and the furniture a quick dusting, and finally sat down in the Adirondack chair shaped like a dolphin on the patio, enjoying the breeze through her hair.

Her father's face flashed quickly before her, and she smiled, silently thanking him for teaching her to be self-sufficient. It had helped her all this time as a single woman. She was proud she could do this all on her own, and had always taken care of herself since her first waitressing job at fourteen. It had been invaluable when her husband had died when Cassie was little, and she was glad she'd taught Cassie the same, shaking her head slowly at how things had turned out for her only daughter.

She was incredibly proud of Cassie and as a mother, she couldn't have hoped for more. Her daughter was happy, confident, self-sufficient, passionate and kind. Had it been naive of her and Annie to think they could offer so many troubled teenager girls an equal opportunity to have a good start in life?

Shaking her head to shove the thoughts away, she leaned back in the chair and took in a deep breath. The smell of the sea washed through her, the salty air reaching her toes. She let the sensation take hold and closed her eyes, intending only to rest for a moment.

Her head jerked up at the sound of Felicia's voice from across the road, saying she'd be over in a few minutes.

She stretched her legs and reached her arms over her head, breathing deeply. She took off her dusty travel clothes and stretched again. Slipping into jeans and a t-shirt, she wrapped a jacket around her waist and slid into her flip-flops. On the way out the door, she grabbed a visor and pulled her shoulder-length, blonde hair into a pony-tail, ready for whatever adventure was next.

CHAPTER 4

*J*ames Dodds tossed his volunteer fireman's hat on the hat rack beside his door as he trudged in from yet another emergency. Thankfully, nobody had been injured during this car crash and he thanked his lucky stars that crisis had been averted. He'd been fortunate during his short time as a bombero—as the volunteer firefighters were called in the South Campos—and they hadn't lost anyone. He hoped their streak of good luck continued forever, and he tugged at his beard as he peered out over the waves.

He'd spent most of his life traveling, and building this house on the cliff looking out over the Sea of Cortez had been his dream come true. Fishing by day, painting by night—it was what he'd worked toward his entire life. And it felt good to have a place—a steady place—to lay his head. Calm and comforting, he felt at peace.

He made himself a cup of tea—not the kind he still dreamed about as a kid from England. But it was all he had and while it wasn't as good as the strong, black tea he'd grown up with, it was comforting. Even when he was a kid and had traveled with his parents, they'd always had a stash of English breakfast tea—usually Earl Grey—and they'd brewed it on camping trips all around the world. If he was going to be in Baja for good, he'd have to scout out a way to replenish his tea.

He walked to the side of his house and reached for a fishing pole. There weren't too many people in camp, and he couldn't help but notice a lovely woman with blonde hair swept up in a ponytail and deep blue eyes walking across the road toward the lovely brick house next door. He'd always admired it, but had decided to build a more common stucco house. But her eyes weren't bright, as he believed everyone's should be when they were surrounded with so much beauty and peace down here at the beach. He wondered why her head was down and her shoulder looked as though they bore the weight of the world.

As he watched her enter the brick house, he hoped for her that the beauty of the sea would calm her, lighten her load as it had for him.

He reached for the fishing pole and hopped in his car, remembering that he'd promised a friend to help him lift some cabinets. There was no more sign of the pretty woman, but as he took off down the beach, he hoped that she would find some happiness.

CHAPTER 5

"Hello," Felicia called through the screen door, Russell in her arms and her quad idling on the road. "You ready to go for a quad ride?"

Megan secured her visor in place and grabbed her sunglasses.

"Sure. I've been dying to see what's for sale in the other campos. We should be able to see the 'for sale' signs if we ride along the beach." She wasn't sure why, exactly, she wanted to see what was for sale. Felicia always said it was just fun to look at what other people had done to their houses as there was a wide range of "tastes" around.

Hopping on her quad, she turned the key, fingers crossed that it would start. It had been sitting in the garage for too long.

"Ah, perfect," she said over her shoulder, as the quad started on the first try. Felicia dropped Russell into the milk crate that was attached to the back of her quad and Megan laughed as the Jack Russell sat quietly, ready for his ride. She followed her friend and the short road to the beach disappeared behind her. The wind in her hair and sun on her skin buoyed her mood, and she felt herself smiling.

They rounded a turn on the beach, heading into a campo north of Playa Luna, following the directions of a 'for sale' sign posted on the beach.

Felicia pulled up short at one of the houses she'd wanted to see. "Let's check this one out," Felicia said, walking toward the beach house. "I think the gate's open."

"We can't do that. It's not like they're having an open house. What if somebody sees us?" Megan asked, not budging an inch off her quad.

"Oh, brother. Come on. Nobody's here, and they want to sell the house." Felicia replied, already walking toward the vacant house.

Megan glanced both ways, up and down the dirt road. "Okay. I guess if they really want to sell the place, visitors are good. I just feel bad we're not buying."

"Well, they'll never know. We might know some-body who knows somebody." Felicia laughed as she peeked in every window of the house.

"True." Megan inched toward one of the windows.

"Wow. Look at that tile in the kitchen. It's beautiful," Felicie said, pressing her nose and hands against the glass window.

Her desire to see the house got the better of her, and she wiped enough dust off the window to see inside. "Wow, that's beautiful. I love the way they did the ceramic tile on the counter, and that sink is gorgeous," she said, peering into the house.

"They have those sinks in town," Felicia said. "The ones with the iguanas and parrots. I like the ones with the fish, those blue and white ones," Felicia said. "I think I'm going to get one for the new house. We can put it in together."

"It wouldn't be that hard, I don't think. We could probably do it," Megan said as her mind turning to that potential project.

"What exactly are you two up to?" a voice called out behind them.

Megan heard herself gasp, and her hands involuntarily came off the glass and raised in the air.

"Put your hands down," Felicia muttered to her friend. "You look ridiculous. What is this, COPS?" She turned toward the voice, smiling.

The man standing on the balcony next door waved toward them. His accent—was it British?—didn't make Megan feel less in trouble, but the twinkle in his eye made her a little less worried.

"Hello, ladies," he said as he leaned on the second-story railing of a neighboring house, staring in their direction.

The man standing on the balcony continued to wave, his wide smile infectious.

"Well, hello," Felicia said, walking toward him. "We're just looking at the house. It's lovely,"

"Yes, it is lovely. They're friends of mine, but they're not here now. I can give you their contact information if you want," he said, taking in Megan's obvious discomfort, his eyes filled with laughter.

"Oh, we're not interested. We're just looking," Megan said, wishing she could get back to her quad and leave.

"My name's James." He started toward them, climbing down the stairs of the balcony.

"Felicia, let's get out of here," Megan whispered, wishing they could just leave.

"Hang on a minute. He's coming to say hello. And he's handsome," Felicia shot back with a grin, clearly enjoying Megan's discomfort.

"You're dating somebody, remember?"

"Yes, I remember. But you're not. Remember?" Felicia said, her voice dripping with glee.

Megan shook her head. The absolute last thing that had crossed her mind in the last several years was the fact that she was single. She had enough to contend with.

"What campo are you ladies from? I think maybe I saw you in my camp earlier. Playa Luna," he said, his eyes resting a moment on Megan as he crossed the sand between them.

"Yes, we're in Playa Luna," Felicia said, extending her hand as they met between the houses. "We really haven't met too many people in our camp. Nice to meet you. I'm Felicia, and this is my friend, Megan."

He turned toward Megan, his hand extended and his eyes curious.

She met his gaze as she shook his hand. His green eyes twinkled, as if he sensed her discomfort. He looked much too young to have the striking white hair and beard, and she found herself curious about him—mildly. Not nearly enough to hang around. She wanted to be in her house, look at the ocean...just rest. She was way too jumpy about just looking at a house.

"No, thank you. We have to go...do something," she said over her shoulder, Felicia's elbow securely in her hands as they got to their quads.

"Something? Okay. Sounds like an emergency," he said, turning back toward his project. "Nice to meet you."

Megan hopped on her quad and started off down the road. As soon as Felicia had Russell in his milk crate, she caught up.

"What was that about?" Felicia asked, her laugh louder than the roar of the quad.

"Shhh," Megan hissed, her finger to her mouth as she tweaked her head in his direction. "We weren't buying. We shouldn't have made anybody think we were."

They sped off, Megan in the lead as she tried to get some distance between them and the embarrassing event. Felicia motioned for Megan to stop as they headed down toward the beach.

"Are you okay?" she said, her eyes dancing. "We have to do *something*? That's the silliest thing I've ever heard. What happened to you?"

"I don't know," Megan said. "I can't believe I did that. I've been so jumpy and nervous lately. I must really need a rest," she said, wiping away tears of laughter. "I must have looked like a complete and total idiot."

"You think?" Felicia said, her laughter ringing. "Too bad for you. He looked just like Sean Connery, and had the accent to boot. You're single, don't forget."

Megan took a look back over her shoulder. "That's the last thing on my mind, friend. Bigger fish to fry with the ranch. I didn't even notice." Her own lie caught her off guard, as she had in fact been curious about him.

"Well, he was really handsome. I thought that's what made you turn into a goof."

"I didn't even really see him. Just wanted to get out of there. Old habits die hard, I guess," she said, continuing to laugh.

"Wow, you've got to lighten up," Felicia said with a laugh. "Maybe a margarita will help."

"Yeah, maybe. I can't handle any more excitement today, anyway."

"Whatever you want, friend," Felicia said as she started her quad and headed toward home.

CHAPTER 6

elicia's house was in complete disarray when they returned, the contents of the Excursion spilled out into the house and patio. Rugs, dishes, curtains and assorted supplies were everywhere as Kyle had set things in the nearest empty space as he unloaded.

"What are those boxes?" Megan asked, pointing to a stack of cardboard lying in the corner.

"Patio furniture, but we have to put it together."

"You didn't tell me that, Mom," Kyle groaned, rolling his eyes. "What else are we going to do? You'd better warn me now."

"Oh, just a few things. You'll be fine. I think I want to go into town tomorrow and get a sink, like that cool one we saw today. I think I need the one with the fish on it," she said, glancing in her unfinished bathroom.

"It would go great with the shower curtain I just brought down."

"Well, whatever. I have to go visit the doctor, anyway, and see when he'll let me volunteer. Make a list and we can tackle it tomorrow," Kyle said over his shoulder as he headed down to the beach with a fishing rod in his hand. "I'm going to try to catch dinner."

"Jeez, remember bringing him down here when he was two? Seems so strange to bring him all grown up and almost a doctor, and have him go off on his own," Megan said, watching Kyle head down to the waves.

"It sure does. And the funny thing is he'll probably bring them home and cook dinner. Fun when they grow up." She smiled as she took some new pots and pans out of boxes and laid them on the counter. "He can use these," she said. "Got a perfect pot to steam clams in. Want to go get some?"

"Absolutely. Let's take an ice chest and some margaritas. We can have some while we're digging. You get that, and I'll go get the forks and the basket."

She started down the small sand dune toward her house, trying her best to keep the thoughts at bay. They seemed to haunt her constantly, her need to make a decision an ever-present ball of worry. Shaking her head, she hurried through the sand and over the dirt road to her house, the reds and yellows of the ladrillo brick catching her eye in contrast with the blue of the water beyond. It really was a beautiful place to be, and if you had to think a problem through, there wasn't anywhere better.

She grabbed the clam basket, the digging forks and an empty five-gallon water bottle to fill up with salt water.

"Perfect timing," she said as Felicia pulled up in the Jeep. Throwing the supplies in the back next to the thermos of frosty margaritas, she hopped in.

"Yum, that's going to be great. Too bad they won't be cleaned out enough to have later when Cassie comes. Let's get a lot, and we can have them tomorrow for an appetizer and maybe even make clam linguini." She was excited to be down on the rock point again, and she could almost taste the sweet butter clams just thinking about them.

"You know I don't cook. I'll dig as many clams as you want, but you have to do something with them," Felicia said.

"I don't know how you raised Taylor and Kyle without ever cooking."

"Yes, you do. You did it for me. When you weren't cooking, it was noodles and broccoli at my house," Felicia said, reminding her friend that they had gotten through raising their toddlers together.

"Or nachos," Megan said, fondly remembering the kids, so close in age, and how much time they'd all spent together then. She had been a stay-at-home mom then, and Felicia was working. Megan had all the kids during the day, and they'd grown up like brothers and sisters. They were still all very close, Cassie and Taylor both living and working in San Diego, and fishing together with Kyle at any opportunity.

Felicia drove down to the beach, Russell sitting in her lap as the milk crate was filled with digging supplies. He was small, but a real trooper and took his assignment as mascot during this clam-digging trip as seriously as he could, usually until the first seagull flew by and he chased it up the beach.

As soon as they started out, a new, huge house caught her eye. It was situated right on the cliff over-looking the sea just like hers. It had two garages and two stories with a big balcony. She could swear it hadn't been there last time she visited, but she had to confess that trip had been a whirlwind so she might not have noticed. The remaining houses quickly flashed by as they drove down the beach, headed toward the rock point that was exposed only at low tide. Twice a day, every day, it was covered in water and inaccessible as the tide crawled toward the cliffs just south of Playa Luna. Now, though, the rocks were exposed, and clamming would be easy.

As Kyle came into view, he flagged them down, smiling broadly. "Check this out. Four corvina already, pretty good-sized ones. Should be plenty for fish tacos." He had been fishing off the shore for only a while, and seemed very pleased that he'd caught so many already.

"Your father would be so proud," Felicia said with a

wave as she started the jeep again and headed for the point.

"He seems really happy," Megan said, glad that he seemed to be finding his place in the world.

"Remember when we bailed him out of jail for his graffiti gifts all over town?" Kyle had had a bit of a rough time in high school and hadn't gone straight to college. He'd spent a fair amount of time down at the beach and somehow found his way to volunteering with the local doctor and that was all it took.

"Oh, gosh, how could I possibly forget? I almost killed him," she said, her hair blowing in the breeze as they ambled south. "Hard to believe he's a doctor. Boggles the mind."

Felicia pulled the jeep up to the point and they both hopped out, grabbing their digging gear and heading off toward the water. They both tried to spot big rocks to sit on while they dug for the tender little clams, keeping none that were smaller than the size of a golf ball.

Golf balls were unfortunately plentiful and Felicia picked up a hot pink one. "I wish these people that hit the golf balls into the water at high tide would come and collect them at low tide. They're all over."

"Free balls for you, my friend," Megan said, acknowledging Felicia's love of the game. "We can pick those up, too, and you can keep them."

"I didn't think of that. Good plan," she said as they settled down on their rocks to dig.

Megan got right into it, excited to have clams again after such a long time. Removing the top layer of rocks and exposing wet sand below, she let out a little squeak as little crabs scattered everywhere.

"Make sure they don't crawl up your legs. That happened to me one time and it bit me in the butt."

"Ouch. I've only had one grab onto my toe and not let go, and that really hurt. Wouldn't want one up my shorts," Megan said, laughing at the memory.

Grabbing their forks and digging down about three inches, they quickly pulled clams out of the sand and threw them in the basket.

"How's Cassie doing?" Felicia asked as they worked toward their goal. "Haven't heard much since the ground-breaking ceremony."

"She's great. She's ecstatic, actually. Apparently, Alex and Pablo are building them a house that she finally gets to see tonight before they come over, and she said she was hoping we could talk wedding while I'm here."

"Wedding? Wow. I guess they've been engaged for a while and it's time. That's exciting. Do you know how big, how small? When?"

"Last she said is that it should be a year or two off. I guess they changed their minds. Fine by me," she said, tossing the last few clams in the basket. "It'll be nice to see them tonight. How's Taylor?"

"She's good. Deep in school and work. I don't see her much with my work schedule, I'm afraid. We talk a lot, but getting together's tough. I asked if she could come this trip but I already knew the answer. Nope."

"Amazing she was able to come with Cassie, then. Was just meant to be. I'm sure she'll be able to get away more when school's out." Megan tossed her last handful of clams in the basket. "Looks like enough to me. What do you think?"

"I have no idea. If you say so, then it is. I'm happy to eat them when you fix them up."

Grabbing the basket now brimming with clams, Megan walked further down to the waves, quickly rinsing the clams off individually in the salt water. She set them aside as Felicia handed her the empty water bottle they'd brought with them. Seawater filled the five-gallon bottle as she held it under the surface, ensuring they'd have enough to soak the clams in overnight, giving the clams the hours needed to clean themselves out as they ingested the corn meal they would sprinkle on top of the water. They were much sweeter that way, and would make an excellent appetizer and linguini.

She heard her stomach growl and realized she hadn't eaten since they'd arrived.

"Since you're taking care of the clams, I'll make my special appetizer for you when we get back." Felicia laughed as she said it, as her friend made her typical response.

"Mm, nachos. Absolutely gourmet," Megan said. They actually sounded good, but she would never let her friend know that. "Just up your alley. Chips and cheese in the oven."

"Hey, I add stuff. Olives and jalapenos and onions."

"You absolutely know how to open cans better than anyone I know. Sounds great," she said, nudging her friend with her elbow. "Honestly, sounds divine. We have arrived in paradise."

CHAPTER 7

*C*assie had barely been able to contain her excitement since she'd gotten the call from her mom first thing this morning. She didn't normally like surprises, but the day had become full of them and she'd decided to just roll with it.

First, Megan had told her she'd be there in the afternoon and right after that, Alex had said she'd finally get to see the house he and his uncle had been building for them. He hadn't let her see a thing in the previous six months—sure, he'd asked her a couple of questions here or there about her preferences, but that was it—and it had been incredibly difficult for her not to sneak up in the dead of night and check it out. She could only imagine what Pablo would come up with. She already loved her mother's house that Pablo had built so many years ago and couldn't imagine how he could do any better.

Alex had insisted that they wait until later in the day and go see the house on the way to visit her mother. It was turning out to be one of the best days she'd had, and when Alex opened the door of the Jeep for her, she hopped right in.

Alex laughed as he turned over the engine. "You seem excited," he said as he headed toward the bluff that the house was built on.

"I think that's an understatement," she said as she rested her hand on his shoulder as he drove. "Best day ever. My mom and Felicia and Kyle are here—which means we'll probably get nachos for dinner—and I get to see my new house. The sanctuary's open, the resort is coming along—what could be better?"

The stunning brick pillars were the first thing Cassie noticed as she neared the beautiful house on the bluff, its arches enclosing a dramatic patio that over-looked the sea. She hadn't been allowed to watch from afar as it grew, brick by brick, but Alex had kept her from seeing more than that until now.

Alex slowed as they came closer, pulling the Jeep to a stop at the bottom of the short road that lead from the beach to the dune. "Wait here a minute," he said, hopping out of the Jeep and jogging toward the house. As he disappeared behind the tall front door, she sighed, her eyes closing as the warm sea breeze caressed her face.

How did I get so lucky? she thought, as the video of the past year played out in her mind, she smiled, remembering her panic when she believed the vaquita would become extinct. Now, thanks to Costa Azul International, the vaquita had their home and were increasing in number for the first time since they'd been discovered. The vaquita had their home, and she had found hers.

Her eyes fluttered, bringing her to the present, a smile dancing on her lips as she surveyed the beautiful, brick house on the bluff. Alex had started back toward the jeep. She had gotten to know him more deeply, and he was no longer able to hide his emotions from her as he once had. As he hurried down the road to her, his excitement and anticipation clearly matched her own.

"Everything is ready for you. You will love it," he said, as he opened her door and held out his hand. His smile was infectious, and Cassie threw her arms around him, laughing.

"Alex, I can't believe you've had this whole house built for us and haven't even let me see it once. How do you know I'll like it?" she asked, drawing back from him.

He took her hand slowly, his lips resting on her palm. "I know your heart, Cassie Lewis, and I know what will make you happy. Come, see our new home," he said, pulling her with him up the road.

They walked up the hill toward the house, comfortable in each other's silence. She was honored he had done this for her, and he had put his heart and soul into it. Planning and building with his Uncle Pablo had been a joy for both of them as they forged their relationship anew, built on respect and love they hadn't had the opportunity to know before.

They drew near the entry of the house, passing through a small patio with a fountain made of colorful Mexican tile, water flowing into a basin on the ground. Brightly colored bougainvillea flowers waved in the breeze as they walked under the shaded roof of the entry.

Alex gestured for her to lead the way toward the front door, his eyes gleaming. Her chin dropped as she looked up at the tall double-entry doors, her hand to her mouth. "Alex, they're beautiful," she gasped, running her fingers over the two dolphin etched deep into the dark mahogany.

"I had them made especially for you," he said as he pushed the door open in front of her. As she passed into the beautiful entry, stunned with its beauty, she was drawn to the four massive windows. The magnetic pull of the view drew her closer, as her gaze was drawn to the beach below.

"Do you like it?" Alex anxiously searching her face. "I hope I haven't made a mistake."

Cassie fell silent, her eyes taking in the view. "I can't believe you did this for me, Alex," she said, her voice quiet. "This is the best gift I've ever received."

His face lit up as he threw open the French doors leading to the patio beyond the beautiful windows. "Come, there's more," he said, reaching for her hand.

They reached the edge of the bluff, and she breathed deeply, taking in the vista. Before her, down the cliff and across the sand, was the breeding sanctuary she had created. As the warm breeze rose from the sea, she rested her head on his shoulder.

"Ah, Cassie," Pablo said, stepping onto the patio, his hat in his hands. He grasped Cassie in a tight hug as she crossed the patio. "Is it to your liking, little one?"

"Pablo, you did this?" she asked, hugging him tightly. "You built a beautiful home for us."

As he lowered his eyes, he said, "I built it for the two of you, yes. But I also built it for Maria and Esteban in their memory." He placed his hat on his head and turned toward the sea. "They would be very proud of what we have done here," he said, turning toward the road. "I know you will be happy here, and we have work to do. Alex, show her the last surprise." Nodding to them both, he disappeared toward the mountains.

Cassie turned to Alex, her eyes searching his face. "More surprises?"

"There's something special that Pablo wanted you to see," Alex said, pulling her toward a wrought-iron metal staircase leading to an upstairs balcony. Close behind him, she climbed the steps.

On the grand terrace overlooking the sea, Alex stood near a large column of brick, shimmering yellow and orange in the disappearing sunlight. She moved closer. "He did all these whale-tails himself?" she said, her hand reaching to touch the brick before her. Her eyes traveled up to the top, and she felt his hand tighten on hers as she surveyed the intricate design in the wall, facing the sea.

"Yes, each one. He did this for you," he said as he admired the expert artistry. As she gazed at the pattern of the moonrise that Pablo had designed with the brick, its rays shooting to all corners of the patio, she turned to Alex, her eyes wet. She thought of how close she had come to believing he would never give it all up for his family. She knew now that he was her rock, her rescuer, and she could rest her heart in his hands and not take on the world alone.

"With all of this love built into the house, how could we not be happy?" She was overwhelmed with gratitude as she turned to the sea, to her sanctuary. "Yes, we will be happy here."

elicia dropped Megan and the clams off at her front door on the way back, and they arranged for Kyle and Felicia to bring the nachos and fish over after a bit. Making quick work of rinsing the clams, she hopped in the shower, letting the hot water flow over her, soothing her, washing off the dust of the trip.

She rummaged through her bag, finding a skirt and top. Slipping the shirt over her head, she was grateful that it was warmer here than at the ranch. She ran a brush quickly through her hair and threw on a little chapstick, satisfied with a glance in the mirror. She quickly brushed on some mascara, her blue eyes standing out against her fair skin.

Flipping her iPod into the player, she hit shuffle, not able to decide what mood she was in. She let the iPod decide for her, and grinned as Bonnie Raitt belted out one of her favorites.

She grinned as she started getting dishes out, preparing for the nacho feast. She opened the refrigerator and reached in for a cold beer. As she popped the top off with her keychain, she heard a voice at the door.

"'Ello, neighbor,"

"Come in, sweetheart. Where's your mom?"

"In England, I believe."

The bottle flew from her hand as she spun to see who was standing in her doorway. It sure wasn't Kyle. Standing in her kitchen was the man from earlier, the spitting image of Sean Connery, but much younger. He even had the accent.

Her face red hot, she bent to pick up the broken shards of glass. He held his hands in front of him as he glanced at her bare feet.

"Stop right there. Don't take a step." She stood frozen to the spot as he bent to pick up the glass, grabbing a small broom and dustpan on the counter. Whisking the glass onto the plastic, he grabbed paper towel to clean up the beer.

"My gosh, I thought you were my friend's son, Kyle."

"Nope, I'm not Kyle," he said, his smile wide. "Hope I didn't disappoint you."

She closed her eyes, willing the embarrassment away. "No, Kyle is my friend's son. I've known him since he was born. Not the man I'm looking for."

"While I am not Kyle, I am, however, building the house two doors down and thought I should introduce myself properly, although we met briefly earlier. James Dodds. How do you do?"

"Megan Lewis, officially," she said. Shaking his hand and catching her breath, she offered him a beer of his own, and grabbed herself another.

"Meg, what a lovely name," he said.

"No, not Meg. Megan," she said. She'd never liked the shortened version of her name. Sounded too light-hearted for her, so she preferred Megan.

"Duly noted," he said with a raised eyebrow as he looked around her house and out onto the cliff.

"I've been wondering who's building that mansion," she said, her balance returning. "Bet the people behind you have made a voodoo doll that looks like you. Their view is disappearing by the day."

"I do feel bad about that...well, sort of," he said with a chuckle. "The view of the sea is what I love most, too. They visit often enough to take in the view." His laughter filled the room. "It wasn't supposed to be as big as it's turned out to be. It looked really small on the napkin in the bar where I drew the plans."

"Oh, you're building it yourself? I haven't been able to make it down for a long time, and haven't seen it since it was just a concrete slab. It's beautiful."

"Thanks. It's my dream come true, my home away from home. Except that it is my home." He walked toward the brick arches framing the view of the Sea of Cortez. "How long have you had this place?"

"I've been coming to Playa Luna for probably thirty years. Finally, about five years ago this house came available and I jumped on it. It's my place to come when I need to breathe."

"I've been coming for the same amount of time. How is it that we've never met?"

"I guess we just travel in different circles," she said. "Or just haven't been here at the same time. I really only know the people that I come down with, my friends across the road."

"Well, you've got a lot of catching up to do, lady," he said, a gleam in his eye. "I'll show you around and introduce you."

Before she could answer, she heard a shout at the door.

"Anybody home?" Felicia walked in holding bags filled with groceries, notably the cans for nachos.

"Well, hello. We meet again," James said, relieving her of her burden and setting the bags on the tile counter.

"Um, hello. What are you doing here?" she asked, glancing curiously from him to Megan and back again, trying to stifle a grin.

"Turns out we're neighbors. What are the odds of that? This must be Kyle," he said, extending his hand toward Kyle and sneaking a glance and a wink at

Megan. "How was the fishing today? The past few days have been pretty good in my books."

"Caught a bunch of corvina. You're an angler?" Kyle put the fish in the refrigerator.

"Absolutely. Nothing I'd rather do, and this is my favorite spot."

Kyle nodded in understanding, and Megan noticed the instant bond between them already that she'd seen hundreds of times between fishermen.

"I noticed something strange today while I was fishing. I've been fishing here with my dad since I was a kid, and only twice have we accidentally caught a totuaba."

"Uh-oh. The forbidden Mexican sea bass," James replied quietly. The huge fish was found only in the Sea of Cortez, and after many years of sport and commercial fishing, they'd been almost decimated. It was a crime to catch them, and people rarely even spoke of them. When they did, they usually whispered.

"Yeah, that's the one. Since I've only seen them a couple of times, I'm not exactly positive, but I'm pretty sure I saw at least three dead ones on the shore today. I was so surprised, I just left them for the turkey vultures."

"That's odd," James replied, tugging lightly on his beard. "Three, you say? Big ones?"

"Yes, they were at least four feet long, each of them. Could feed an entire family really well with each one, and they sure need help down here."

"They were whole? Not just the filet leftovers?"

"No, that's the really strange thing. They were whole, but looked like they'd been gutted. I left well enough alone. I don't need to tangle with the Federales," he said as he gathered up the fish he had caught. "I'll go filet these for fish tacos later. You staying?" he asked James as he opened the door to leave. "We have plenty. Good fishing day. I'll see you guys in a little bit," he said over his shoulder with a tip of his ball cap. "Nice to meet you, James."

A whirling black ball of fur crashed through the open door, running as fast as it could to greet each person in the room.

"Here comes Jimmy," Felicia said, as they all took turns petting the little black dog that always heralded the arrival of the man who'd lived in Playa Luna the longest.

"You know Jimmy?" Megan and James said in unison, as they looked at each other, surprised.

"How can you live here and not know him?" Felicia asked as she opened the bag of tortilla chips and spread them on a baking sheet.

"Hey, all." Jimmy sauntered in after Whiskers, his gray beard framing his wide grin. His worn blue jeans and flip-flops were a familiar sight, and Megan hugged him warmly.

"After all these years, how did we all not meet each other?" James's eyes showed surprise, as he looked from Jimmy to Megan.

"I know everybody. You all just don't know each other," Jimmy said as he hugged Felicia. "Guess you're just not as popular as I am, James."

"I guess not. You seem to know all the lovely ladies."

"That's because I know how to fix stuff when they all get in trouble," he said with a wink. "Good to have somebody around who knows about propane and solar panels."

"Jimmy!" Cassie and Alex came through the door, all smiles.

Megan waited patiently as Cassie hugged Jimmy and Felicia and was introduced to James. When it was finally time for a hug, it lingered as long as she could make it. When she pulled away from her daughter, she had to wipe tears from her eyes. It had been a long time, and so much had happened—to both of them.

Everybody moved onto the patio to watch the sun set and Cassie stayed in the kitchen with Megan when Kyle delivered the fish filets. They fell into an easy rhythm—Cassie had never loved to cook but was a great helper, and that hadn't changed—while they chatted.

"So, a wedding sooner rather than later?" Megan asked as she handed Cassie the bowl of batter for the fish.

"Oh, Mom, yes, sooner. Alex took me to the house he and Pablo built for us and it's gorgeous. I can't wait for you to see it. It's all ladrillo, just like this one. I'm anxious to get in."

"Sounds beautiful," Megan said after Cassie had described it even more. "I can't wait to see it."

Cassie dipped the breaded fish filets into the hot oil, moving them around as her mom had taught her and Megan nodded in satisfaction.

"Can you come over tomorrow? Maybe tomorrow night? We can set some tables up on the patio. All of you can come. And we can talk more about the wedding."

"Sounds perfect. Go ahead and invite everybody while I carry this stuff out. I can't wait."

Megan watched her daughter invite everyone to the first party at her new house—that she didn't even live in yet. She hadn't seen her this excited since she was little, and it warmed her heart.

The evening turned into a bit of a party, and several other neighbors stopped by. Megan met lots of people, including James's friend Colin. He was a volunteer firefighter for the south campos, and Megan also learned that James was a volunteer as well. There was no formal fire station, and the south campos relied on volunteer residents, but it was pretty rigorous training, she found out.

Felicia's nacho's were a hit. They ate on the patio, and Megan served the famous San Felipe fish tacos that she and Cassie had made to a very appreciative audience.

"These are delicious." James was clearly enjoying his tacos, as Kyle beamed with pride at his catch.

"Nothing quite like fish this fresh." Kyle helped himself to another fish taco, smothering it with cabbage, tomatoes, onions and the all-important white sauce that made them so special.

"How do you make your white sauce? It's better even than what they have in town," James asked, between bites.

Jimmy pushed himself back from the table as he finished his beer.

"I can guarantee she won't tell you. I've been trying to get it out of her for years."

She felt her cheeks warm at the compliment, and was pleased that everybody enjoyed their tacos.

"You're right. I can't tell you or I'd have to kill you."

"Hey, I don't want to know," Felicia chimed in. "If I knew how, I'd have to do it."

As the laughter died down, everyone said their goodbyes, and Megan found herself standing on the porch with James. The moon had yet to appear on the horizon and the stars dotted the black velvet of the sky.

"I realize I just met you, but several times tonight you seemed very far away." He leaned against the brick pillar of the porch, making no effort to leave with the others.

Megan swallowed hard as the memory of the ranch came flooding back. She had been trying to forget, and thought she had masked her anxiety pretty well tonight, attempting to enjoy the company.

"I just have a lot on my mind, I guess." She looked

out over the desert, wishing that she knew what to do to make it better.

"Whatever it is, you can decide what you want, and you can decide to be happy."

"It's not that easy." She felt her stomach tighten at the thought of the decision she needed to make.

"Sure it is. Just choose happy. Whatever that means for you."

He turned and headed toward his house. "Thank you for a lovely evening," he said over his shoulder as he disappeared into the darkness.

CHAPTER 9

hoose happy? She thought as he disappeared. What did that even mean? She'd been responsible since the day she started working, and before that as the oldest child in her family, helping out with the younger kids. She'd raised one of her own, keeping her life together when Cassie's father died when Cassie was young. A single mom after that, each increasingly responsible job had meant a better salary, and the decisions to take the jobs were no-brainers. It wasn't until she'd missed most of her daughter's games and events that she realized she was working more than she should. But it was what the job required, wasn't it? What choice did she have?

The opportunity to start the girls ranch had seemed like an escape, at least one step closer to happy. She'd tried. Owning her own business and working with her trusted sister had sounded like a dream come true. Unfortunately, it had turned into something else.

Cassie was out of the house, in college, and she had been single longer than she'd been married. Her parents lived there, and her dad had been ill. The thought of being closer made the whole package ideal. Besides, if it didn't work out, she could just get a job again.

She'd taken the money she had saved for retirement and invested in the ranch, passionate about helping teen foster girls and providing a safe place for them to live, to grow, to heal. It was what she had done her whole career – help people. Previous students were her friends on Facebook, and she enjoyed seeing people help themselves and be productive.

She decided to stop thinking for the day and try to relax. She'd taken a bath with her bubbles and candles after everyone had left, hoping it would help her sleep. Even in her favorite bedroom, the warm ladrillo bricks surrounding her and the waves lapping at the shore, sleep had been elusive. She'd tossed and turned, the words, "Choose happy," running through her mind, unbidden. If it were that easy, wouldn't everybody just choose to be happy? *A ridiculous idea,* she thought to herself as she gave up on sleep, looking forward to the sunrise.

Shaking the thoughts from her head, she grabbed her San Felipe jacket emblazoned with colorful fish and threw it on over her silk pajama pants. She looked down, realizing that the yellow jacket and the purple silk pants were going to be as vivid as the sunrise. Add to that the lime green scarf that was closest to her, she thought anybody would need sunglasses to be around her.

After years of hanging out with Felicia, she knew her friend would be snoring away and wouldn't be up for hours, so it was probably a safe bet that she wouldn't be teased by her. She pulled her black Uggs on, laughing at herself, not caring what she looked like as she anticipated a beautiful sunrise. Filling the kettle with water, she placed it on the stove, set a mug on the counter and threw in a tea bag.

While she waited for the water to boil, she settled into her favorite Adirondack chair perched right on the cliff. The birds were starting to wake up, pelicans and seagulls clinging to the shore as if at the starting line, ready to begin their day of searching for fish.

As the sky lightened, her gaze was drawn to its pink hue. A few clouds clung to the horizon, and as the sun peeked over the water, the clouds blazed with orange and red. She closed her eyes, feeling peaceful and serene.

"Beautiful, isn't it?" she heard behind her, a vaguely familiar voice breaking into her reverie.

She turned in her chair and found herself gazing into the same piercing eyes she had seen last night. James stood directly behind her and he was staring at her, his eyes bright.

"Yes, it's the most beautiful sunrise I think I've ever seen," she said, turning back toward the water. The sun had risen completely now, and the rays were shimmering on the waves.

"Yes, the sunrise is beautiful, too," he said, his eyes remaining on her.

Startled, she turned toward him, her face as crimson as the sky. It had been ages since she'd been remotely aware of a handsome man, and her stomach tightened as she turned away.

"I couldn't help but notice you out here. Your pajamas rivaled the sunrise." He smiled, looking down at his own multi-colored Hawaiian shirt, jeans and Uggs. "It seems we have similar taste in fashion."

She glanced down at her vivid array of clothes, not believing that on all the days she would grab whatever clothes were closest, this would happen. "You certainly can't mean that with this get-up on," she said.

"It certainly is worthy of a second glance."

"You're up early." Not being a quick thinker in embarrassing situations, it was the best she could do, cringing at her lack of witty one-liners.

"I find this time of the morning to be especially peaceful, and I saw you out here. I hope you don't mind."

"No, not at all."

The sound of the kettle whistling rang from the kitchen, gratefully giving her something to say next. "I put the kettle on. Would you like some tea?"

"Tea? Did you say tea? I thought all Americans drink coffee in the morning."

"Not me. I love tea, Earl Grey to be exact. Will that do?"

"Oh, a civilized woman in Baja at last," he said, as he followed her into the house. "Should be a right start to the day, then."

She smiled as she handed him his mug, watching as he held it under his nose with his eyes closed. "I haven't had proper tea in ages. Can't get it down here. This is wonderful. Thank you," he said as he spooned brown sugar into his mug. "And a spot of cream, if you have it?"

She took the cream from the refrigerator, handing it to him. "So, you're British, then?" she asked as she poured some cream in her tea as well.

"Born there, and moved to Canada as a lad. Moved back and forth several times. My father had the travel bug, and we lived lots of places."

"I've never been to England, but I was a British Literature major in college. I love all things British," she said.

"Really? Now that's good to know," he said, laughing as he walked back out onto the cliff.

As he laughed, she realized what she had just said. "Oh, I didn't mean..." she sputtered, almost spilling her tea.

"It's okay. I know what you meant." He sat down, peering up into the sky directly above. "Look up."

She followed the sound of a jumble of squawks, looking up to see a very long lines of seagulls flying by. Several birds formed a V in the front of the line, and occasionally they would call back to the back of the line.

James laughed. "We call them the Mexican Navy. Not sure why," he said, shielding his eyes from the sun that had made its appearance over the horizon.

"The seagulls? Because of the formation?" She'd never noticed before that they shared the burden, some leading for a while before letting others forge ahead.

"Yes. It's hard work being in the front, and they can only do it for so long. Then they go to the back and rest. A real team effort. None of them ever have to do the work alone."

"Hm," Megan said, thinking of her work at the girls' home. They did have a team and they were all in it together. And so many girls were better for it. She was quite proud of what they'd done, she realized. It was hard work, but the rewards very much worth it.

"That's amazing," Megan said finally, feeling lucky she had just witnessed that.

"Pretty funny, isn't it? What a place, birds in military formation."

"Do you get to see things like that all the time?" she said, her eyes wide, thinking of her city life.

"If you stay long enough, the gifts of nature will

astound you. Truly remarkable." He stood, taking the final sip of his tea. "Some of these moments beg to be captured and the camera doesn't quite do it justice."

Megan nodded. "I've always wished that I could capture some of the things I've seen, too."

"You could," James said as he cocked his head and looked at her.

"No, I can't do that."

"Do what? Create? You just do what you feel."

"Feel? Art? I can't even draw stick people," she said, laughing at herself. "I had an art teacher give me an F on a travel poster because I made the tulips blue. He said there aren't any blue tulips. I never drew anything again."

"That's horrible. Of course, there are blue tulips if they exist in your head. Anything goes," he said. "Just do whatever you feel."

Megan turned back out to the water. She was so busy thinking, and talking to people and working that she seldom really knew what she felt, certainly not in the context of creating art. She just reacted, tried to put out fires. Anything beyond that would be a luxury.

James seemed to be thinking for a moment as he'd gone quiet. Megan assumed he was watching the sky turn colors until he turned to her.

The sky was spectacular, multiple shades of blue and yellow and pink streaking the sky. The beauty and serenity of the moment struck her, and she wondered if this was what it was like to feel like you could be happy, create something. She thought maybe she'd caught a glimmer, and it felt foreign to her as she turned to go inside.

"Thank you for the tea, Megan. And the entertainment," he said, glancing at her outfit.

She laughed as he headed for the door. "Sure, any time."

"That would be nice," he said. "I'll see you tonight at Cassie's, if not before."

She was startled for a moment as she'd forgotten Cassie had invited James to join them at dinner the night before. Not that she was disappointed.

"Oh, all right. You know where it is?"

"Sure. I drive by there quite frequently and have seen it going up, along with all the progress at the resort. I'm looking forward to it."

She watched him for a moment as he headed down the dirt road toward his house and realized that she actually was looking forward to seeing him again.

CHAPTER 10

"*F*elicia, get up," Megan said as she barged into Felicia's house. She'd almost run across the road, hoping that James wouldn't see her. Either way, it wasn't possible to look calm, cool and collected in her neon outfit.

"What? What? Don't talk to me until you put coffee on," Felicia said as she pulled the covers over her head.

She grabbed the coffee pot and filled it with water. She knew her friend would be no good to her until she could at least smell coffee. Grabbing the coffee can, she measured the right amount in the filter and hit the on button before heading back into the bedroom.

"I don't smell it yet," Felicia said from under the covers. "What time is it, anyway?"

"I don't know. I think it's around seven o'clock. Maybe."

"What the heck? I don't think I've been up this early since...well, a long time."

The coffee started dripping into the pot, making its coffee noises. "See, it's coming. Can you hear it? You missed a great sunrise."

"I can hear it, but I can't smell it. And what normal person watches sunrises, anyway? That's still night time in my book."

"You'll smell it in a minute. Get up," Megan said, tugging at the covers.

"What is it?" Felicia said, as she sat up, her eyes still closed. "Ah, I think I can smell it. I think I can open my eyes, now," she said, opening one first. As she looked at Megan, both eyes flew open wide, her hand flying to her mouth to stifle her laughter.

"What the heck are you wearing?" she said, barely able to suppress her giggles.

"What? Oh, whatever. It's all I had handy."

Felicia put her hands over her eyes. "Oh, my gosh. I think I just saw the sunrise. In neon. Grab some coffee for me. I think I've been blinded."

"Oh, come on," Megan said, laughing. In the kitchen, she poured the magic elixir for her friend, hoping it would get her out of bed so she could tell her the news.

She waited for her to get one sip down, knowing it would go easier if she did. "Okay, that's all you get. Guess what?"

"You went color blind overnight?"

"Very funny. No, I didn't. I couldn't sleep, got up in the dark and just put this on. Get over it."

"I'm not sure I can. But, go on. What happened?"

"I was sitting watching the sunrise and that guy came over."

"That guy? The one from yesterday? The Sean Connery guy?" She actually looked a little interested now, and she got out of bed and pulled on a sweatshirt over her pajamas.

"You don't look any better than I do, my friend. Nice sweatshirt and pajamas."

"Hey, at least they're in the same section on the color wheel," she said, straightening her hair and pulling on her slippers. "So spill. What happened?

Megan poured herself a cup of coffee, grabbing the French vanilla creamer from the refrigerator and poured a splash in the mug.

"I couldn't sleep at all, even after my goddess bath. I woke up before the sun came up. I was watching the sunrise and he just came over."

"And he stayed after he saw you in that get-up?" She looked at her friend over the rim of her mug as she drank her coffee quickly.

"Yes, he did. He even said I was beautiful. At least, I think he did," she said.

"Wow, you're kidding me? That's awesome."

"Is it? Felicia, I haven't been interested in a man in ages. Too busy working. I don't even know what to say, and I keep saying pretty stupid things."

"Well, yes, you do, but he seems to like you anyway."

"That's not very nice," Megan said, stepping on her friend's foot as she walked over to the window.

"Ouch. Stop it. I'm just kidding."

"I know. It's just so foreign to me. Said he was looking forward to seeing us tonight at Cassie's. I'd forgotten that she'd invited him." Megan squirmed a bit in her chair.

"Looking forward to seeing you, you mean. You're the one he came to visit this morning." she said. She looked into her empty mug and lurched toward the coffee pot, pouring herself another cup. "Ahh. Getting better."

Megan laughed at her friend. Her morning coffee addiction was legendary, and Megan was grateful that she was even capable of this level of conversation with her best friend before cup number three.

"I don't think so. I just think I happened to be up this morning, so he stopped in."

"Whatever. You think that if you want to, but I saw how he looked at you last night. When you were showing him around the house, he stood in your bedroom for a while and said, 'So this is where you sleep?' Remember?"

"Yeah, I remember. What of it?"

"That's not a normal thing people say. He was flirting."

"He was not." Her stomach tightened at the thought. It hadn't even occurred to her that he might be flirting.

"Oh, yes, he was. I meant to tell you today, anyway, but it seems he beat me to you."

She stared out the window, looking out to the ocean. "Well, he doesn't know much about me yet, so it will be a short-lived flirtation, if he's even interested." She lowered her eyes and leaned her forehead against the glass. "Hey, a lot of guys would want a woman who is losing a business, soon to be unemployed, and lives in a different country."

"Oh, come on. Nobody thinks that about you but you. You're going to land on your feet. You always do."

"Thanks, Flee. I need to think that. Not sure what I'm going to do."

"Well, for today, just go with it. Forget about all that, and be happy."

Megan's mouth dropped open, and she turned toward her friend. "That's exactly what he said."

"Well, then it's a message. One not to be ignored."

Megan stood and looked out over the water. "I think maybe I'll write in my journal a little bit today. I haven't done that in a long time. Oh, wait, you wanted to go into town."

Felicia stood and stretched, the caffeine apparently now in her veins.

"I don't mind. I'll take Kyle. He wants to go in and talk to the doctor anyway, and I want to get a new sink."

"Okay, if you're sure you don't mind. I don't really

want to go to town anyway. Don't forget to be back for dinner at Cassie's, though."

"Oh, right," Felicia said as she poured another cup of coffee. "We'll be back in plenty of time. Are you cooking? Cassie doesn't know how, which I'm sure you remember."

Megan laughed. "She didn't ask me to, so maybe we're going to the restaurant or something. I'm not going to worry about it."

Felicia's eyebrows rose. "Well, that's a first. You not worrying about something like that. Well done. Maybe there's hope for you after all."

Just as Megan headed off the porch, James walked up the dune toward Felicia's door.

"Mornin', Felicia," James said as he nodded in her direction. "And hello again, Megan."

Felicia smiled in Megan's direction and nodded.

"Can I get you some coffee?" she asked.

James shook his head. "No, thanks. I've already had my fill of the best tea I've tasted in months."

Taking a quick glance at Felicia, Megan saw she was trying not to laugh.

"Megan, I was wondering if you'd like to stop by a little later this morning. We were talking earlier about art, and creativity and there are some things I'd like to show you."

"Uh, I guess so," Megan said slowly.

He smiled and pointed to her clothes. "I thought

that with your sense of color and style, you might be interested in seeing some of my art."

Megan closed her eyes and cringed as Felicia literally spit out some of her coffee and coughed.

"Sure, sure, that would be great," she said quickly, hoping James hadn't noticed. He was already walking back to his house and she was relieved that he hadn't, in fact, seemed to notice.

As he crossed the road and was out of earshot, Felicia said, "Your sense of style and color? Okay. I am right and you are wrong. He's flirting. And he wants to show you his art collection." Her friend wiggled her eyebrows again over the top of her mug.

Megan sighed and wondered how she felt about that, if it was even true. She decided she didn't care one way or the other—he was interesting and handsome and it was something to do. She was supposed to just relax, and it sounded like a good way to do it.

"I'm not going to talk about this anymore. Have fun in town," she said, putting an end to the conversation. At least for now.

CHAPTER 11

*M*egan spent some time writing in her journal as she sat on the deck. The waves crashing against the shore spurred her along, and before she knew it she'd written pages and pages of memories she had from being at the beach. She'd just written about as many times she could think of that she'd been happy, and although not many of them were particularly recent, there were quite a few. Maybe she just needed to remember what that felt like, and change things up so she could feel that way again.

She glanced at her watch and thought it was probably time to go over to James's house. She'd changed her clothes earlier for everyone's benefit, and had pulled on a comfortable black skirt and powder blue top. She slid into her flip flops and before she headed out the door, she reached into the fridge for a container of the white sauce she had left over from the evening before. James had said he liked it, so it was all she could think of to bring with her.

She walked down the dirt road toward his house and started up the steps. They were tiled with the terra cotta colored saltillos that everyone loved and the risers had colorful tile all along them, in beautiful shades of green, yellow, orange, blue in lots of different patterns. A hammock hung from two posts on the porch. She rapped lightly on the French door, shifting from foot to foot. She had absolutely no reason to be nervous—she was an adult with grown children, for goodness sake—but she was nervous nonetheless.

James opened the door wide and gestured for her to come in. She smiled as she did and looked around the large room, a sweeping bank of French doors on the water side providing a fantastic view.

"This is beautiful," she said. "What a great job you've done."

"Thank you," he said as he took the container she held out to him. "For both things. The compliment and the white sauce. I meant it when I said I'd never had better."

"You're welcome." She slowly walked toward the kitchen, admiring the huge kiva fireplace in the center of the room. "Wow, what a great kiva," she said as she ran her hand along the curved edges and peered into the main part of it. It looked like a beehive in the center of the room.

"Thanks, I love it. In the winter, it heats the entire downstairs."

"I bet that's lovely," she said. She loved her wood stove for the same reason, but his fireplace was huge, and a centerpiece of the room.

"Let me give you a tour," he said, and he took her hand, leading her from room to room. "The bedroom's not quite finished but you have to see it anyway."

In each room, there were beautiful paintings—some of the ocean, some of boulders, some of mountains. They were beautiful, very colorful and quite large. He also had hung other kinds of pieces of art that looked like they might be from exotic places—not that she'd been to many—but she was pretty positive that some of the ceramic plates, metal art and African masks hadn't been from the states.

"You have some exquisite pieces," she said. "You must have traveled quite a bit."

"I did. I've worked for various magazines over the years and was fortunate enough to see many countries, many continents."

It didn't surprise her at all that he was well-traveled. Somehow, in the back of her mind, maybe that went along with being happy. And being adventurous, and brave enough to try new things.

She gasped as he led her up the stairs and she entered into a large, square room, French doors on three sides. There were too balconies and he pulled her out onto the one that faced the water.

"Wow," she said slowly. "You can see forever."

He laughed. "And I feel the same way," he said, pointing to the chair and telescope at the end of the balcony. "The stars and the moonrise—I could look at them forever."

"I can see why you'd never want to leave." Megan could tell that he had the same affection for Playa Luna that she had—only he was fortunate to be there much more frequently than she was.

She stopped in the stairwell on the way back downstairs, pausing to look more closely at one of the many paintings. This one was of what looked like tide pools, but was just in black and white. Charcoal, maybe? All of the other scenes were in vivid color.

"This is beautiful. All of the shades of gray—I love it."

"Ah, shades of gray," he said. "That's one of my favorites, too. I sketched that in San Diego once when I was visiting a friend."

She turned and stared at him, her mouth open.

"You—you did this?"

He sat down on the step and looked out over the downstairs. "Yes. I did all of these."

"Well, with the exception of these two," James said, stopping before two rather small, extremely colorful paintings of donkeys. "Two of the kids at the poblado did these."

"The kids? At the local school?"

James cleared his throat and kept moving. "Yes. I

teach them art there, once a week. They're getting pretty good."

She stopped in her tracks and looked around. As a single mom and bread-winner, it hadn't ever occurred to her to try to paint something. "Wow, they're fantastic," she said again as she plopped down on the step below his. "I can't even imagine."

He stood and grabbed her elbow, pulling her up beside him and guiding her downstairs. "Well, we'll see about that. That's what the kids said, too, before they tried."

He pulled her to the far end of the house and opened a door, guiding her down steps into what looked like a work room. Easels stood to the side, and benches with paints and paintbrushes lined the walls.

"It's a hobby of mine. I thought after our earlier conversation maybe you'd like to try it, too. You can even paint a blue tulip if you like."

She turned quickly toward him, looking up into twinkling eyes.

"Really?"

"Sure. Why not? No reason why you can't, no matter what your teacher said long ago."

He gestured to a stool in front of an easel that held a blank white canvas. "You can just do whatever you want, or I'm happy to teach you a thing or two."

She pulled her hair back and sat on the stool, a laugh threatening to escape in between the rapid beats of her heart. She reached with a sweaty palm toward one of the brushes and took a deep breath.

"I think I'd like to paint that blue tulip after all," she said and he nodded with encouragement.

"A blue tulip it shall be," he said as he sat beside her.

She couldn't remember laughing so much in years and years as he nudged and prodded her into courage to actually put paint on the canvas. While they painted, she asked him question after question about his life, his travels. The stories were fascinating—he'd even sailed from California to Tahiti as crew on a boat.

"That was long, long ago. I started traveling at a very young age," he said.

She paused for a moment and looked at him.

"Were you trying to find something, or get away from something?" she asked.

He stroked his beard. "I'm not sure. But my hair turned white when I was thirty—so maybe a bit of both."

She couldn't help herself with the next question.

"Never married? No family?"

He shook his head. "Nope. Some relationships here and there, but I never found quite the right one," he said as he reached for more paint.

She was having a marvelous time painting and listening. He never once made her feel like she couldn't do it, and after a couple of hours—but what seemed like minutes to her—he stood and took a step back.

"What fine work you've done, Megan. Museum quality, certainly."

She poked her elbow into his ribs and laughed.

"Ouch. I wasn't kidding. I'd be proud to hang it anywhere," he said.

"I'm not sure I'm brave enough to hang it anywhere." Megan stood back and looked at it, too. She supposed it wasn't all that bad, although she still thought she'd get an F in art class. But it was a pretty color, and the blue tulips were peaceful to look at. She wouldn't mind hanging it in her bedroom, maybe, where nobody would see it but her.

"Oh, it's getting late and I need to be at Cassie's a little early. I told her I would be, so I have to go," she said.

James bowed slightly and reached for her painting. "I'll carry it home for you. Make sure you don't touch it until it's dry. And thank you for spending the day with me. It was lovely."

"It was," Megan said. "I can't thank you enough for encouraging me to do this. It felt—it felt really good."

"Ah, just the beginning. You have so many things you could explore. This is but one."

She took in a deep breath as he escorted her to her house.

"Hm. Well, I won't be here long enough to do much more of this, I'm afraid. So thank you for showing me."

"Ah, what a pity," James said with a frown. "Well, I

think I'll see if Kyle would like to throw a line in the water before we head over to Cassie's."

"I'm sure he'd love to. And thanks again for the painting lesson."

"My pleasure," James said as he set the painting inside the door of Megan's house. "See you tonight."

Megan laughed—fishermen were all alike. Compulsive, and not much time for anything else. She found it intriguing that he found time to teach the kids at the local school and wondered what more she didn't know about him as he walked away.

CHAPTER 12

*M*egan was right—Cassie'd had the dinner catered from the resort restaurant. When Megan arrived, plates of tamales, enchiladas, tacos, chips and salsa were set out on tables with colorful tablecloths billowing in the breeze, just like the groundbreaking ceremony. She wasn't at all surprised, and was actually happy that her daughter was so resourceful for someone who didn't like to cook. Besides, it meant she had more time to just talk to people and enjoy the beautiful evening.

Cassie and Felicia had driven up to the resort together, and Kyle and James had said they'd follow. When they'd left, the men were on the beach, barefoot, their fishing poles floating on the waves. They clearly weren't ready to leave yet, and Megan didn't mind just some girl time with her daughter. She instinctively knew that there was more that Cassie wanted to talk about, and she was looking forward to hearing what it was.

"I'm so glad you're here, Mom," Cassie said after she'd given Megan and Felicia a tour of the house. There wasn't much to do to get ready for dinner, and Megan wasn't quite sure what to do with herself if she wasn't cooking. She and Felicia followed Cassie out onto the patio where the caterers were setting up, walking out toward the edge of the bluff. The sky was starting to turn, and as they sat and looked out over the water, Cassie caught them both up on the sanctuary. She pointed to where it was, and Megan was thrilled with the progress. The pride and sense of accomplishment her daughter radiated warmed her heart.

"Sweetheart, I'm so proud of you. I thought for sure that it was all over when the resort owners said no."

Felicia laughed. "Who knew the resort owner would fall in love with Cassie and the vaquita, too?"

"Not me," Cassie said, handing her mother a glass of wine. "Alex made this all possible and I'll never forget it."

Megan reached for her daughter's hand. "It's obvious how much he loves you, Cassie. All is well with the world."

"My world, anyway. How about yours?"

Megan sighed and leaned back in her chair. It has always been difficult for her to know how much to tell her daughter. They'd been through some pretty rough times, and her instinct was to protect Cassie from worrying about her own mother. No child, even in their thirties, should have to worry if their mother was going to be all right. Besides, the truth of the matter was that Megan had taken a pretty big risk with her retirement and she wasn't feeling like that was the most brilliant thing she'd ever done. As sad as it was, it was embarrassing.

Felicia nudged her knee and they exchanged a glance when Felicia nodded at her.

"Things aren't going real well," Felicia said, making Megan's choice for her.

Without going into too much detail, Megan gave Cassie an overview of the situation of the ranch.

"Please don't say I told you so," she finished.

"Oh, Mom, I would never, ever say that. You were—are—as passionate about helping people as I was about helping the vaquita. I understand completely, but I'm very, very sorry it isn't working out."

"Me, too, sweetheart," Megan said as she hugged her daughter.

"When will you know what's going to happen? You know you always have a place with us here if you need it. And even if you don't. I'd love to have you down here or in Playa Luna full time."

Megan was startled by the comment. Even with the possibility of the ranch going under, it hadn't occurred to her to live in Playa Luna, although her brick house was pretty much all she had left.

"I couldn't possibly. I have to work somewhere. Can't do that here."

Cassie smiled at Felicia. "Felicia, tell Mom that with the resort going up, and scaling back from the five-star concept and going more eco-tourism, I'm sure we could find a great position for Mom. Something she'd even be passionate about." Turning to Megan, she said, "You love kayaking. And paddle boarding. Maybe you could be an instructor."

Megan's mouth dropped open and Felicia laughed.

"Your mom loves it, yes, but she can only stay upright on the paddle board half the time. I don't think instructing people on how to fall off is what you want."

Cassie laughed and leaned back in her chair. "Well, okay, maybe not that. But Mom, seriously consider it. Please."

Megan shook her head slowly. "I appreciate your kindness, Cassie, but I'm sure I'll land on my feet. I always do."

"Have you told them the good news?" Alex said as he breezed onto the patio and sat on the arm of Cassie's chair. He wrapped his arm around her and kissed the top of the head.

"Um, no, we haven't gotten to that yet," Cassie said.

Megan noticed that her daughter's cheeks had turned a little pink and her eyes were bright as she looked up at Alex.

"Mom, you said you guys are staying through next weekend, right?"

Felicia nodded. "Yep. We both lucked out and got time off."

Alex smiled and stood up, pulling Cassie up to stand beside him. He wrapped his arm around her waist as if to encourage her, and Megan wondered what was up.

"Mom, now that the house is done, Alex and I want to get married as soon as possible."

"Oh, that's fantastic," Megan said. She stood and hugged both Alex and Cassie, thrilled that her daughter was moving on with her decision. "Felicia and I can spend the next week and a half planning the wedding with you. The colors, the dress, the food--all of it. It's perfect timing."

Cassie and Alex exchanged glances.

"Mom, I don't want a big wedding. I hope you don't mind. We just want to get married, and we want to do it here. Next Saturday, before you leave."

"I...well, that's soon. There's a lot to be done." Megan took a glance at Felicia, who shrugged her shoulders.

"Not really. Once we decided, and after seeing how easy it was to cater this party tonight, we just want to do it. I don't care about colors, or my dress, or any of that. I just want to be married to the man I love."

Alex radiated joy as he kissed Cassie's hand. "I feel the same. And my parents are available next weekend, you all are here, it's perfect."

Cassie clapped and bounced a little. "I even checked

with Taylor and she can take off work to be my maid of honor. It's perfect. All my favorite people are here, and I say we just do it."

"Sounds perfect to me," Kyle said as he and James stepped onto the porch. "I won't be able to get any more time off until my residency is over and I wouldn't want to miss the event of the year."

Cassie hugged Kyle and rested her palm on his cheek. "I wouldn't want to do it without my honorary brother in attendance. Thanks, Kyle."

"Well, it's settled, then," James said. "An auspicious occasion, no doubt, and an excuse for another party."

"Oh, my gosh, I can't wait," Felicia said. She hesitated for a moment and looked down at her shorts and flip flops. "Is it going to be casual?"

"Of course," Alex said. "The most important thing is that we'll all be together."

Megan couldn't believe it. She'd thought she was just coming down to rest and relax, but it was turning out that she'd be having a family event after all. She would dearly love Annie and Daniel to be there, but there was no way they could leave the girls' home, and she knew they'd understand.

After hugs all around, Cassie and Felicia went inside to check on the caterers and Alex and Kyle went inside for a tour. James came over and sat down beside Megan, who was still absorbing all the new information.

"Well, this all sounds exciting. I gather you had no

idea they'd do this now." James took a glance back into the kitchen. "It's clear they're in love. Can't miss it. And I suppose at that age, they're eager to get on with their lives together."

Megan nodded. "I remember vividly what it was like at that age when you meet someone, the right someone, and fall in love. You want to be with them forever, and the sooner the better."

"You miss your husband." James leaned back in his chair.

Megan glanced again at Cassie, who bore a strong resemblance to her father. "At times like this, I wish he was here to see Cassie. He loved her very much, and would be so incredibly proud."

James nodded. "I'm sure he would be. There's a lot to be proud of. And you? Do you miss him?"

"I don't think you can be in love, have an accident take you away from that person and not miss him. I think of him, wonder what it would be like if he hadn't died. That first year, I wasn't sure if I would ever be able to breathe again, let alone have a life. But things eased. It's a fond, distant memory now. Besides, I need to focus on what's in front of me."

"Yes," James said. "And be happy."

Megan rolled her eyes. Here he was again with the happy part. Her daughter was getting married, she was at the beach, and she wasn't sure how much happier she could manage to be, given her current life circumstances.

James cleared his throat and leaned down to pick up a beautiful shell. He rubbed the sand from it and handed it to Megan.

"This is beautiful. I love shells. I always feel bad picking them up, though."

James laughed. "Well, as long as you don't take them all, I think it's all right."

Megan turned the shell over in her hands, rubbing her thumb over the smooth interior that had been worn by being tossed in the sand.

THE PARTY, if you could call it that with the small number of people, lasted long into the night. Everybody chimed in about their opinion of what the wedding should be like until Cassie shook her head and said, "No more talk about the wedding. As long as Alex and I are married at the end of it, I don't care what it is. I'm handing it over to the resort events coordinator and I'm just going to show up."

"Perfect," Megan said, warming to the idea of not being in charge of it and just having fun.

As the party wound down and James announced he was heading home, Megan walked outside with him to get a breath of fresh air.

James turned to her, and his eyes looked to her to be as bright as the stars in the sky.

"I've been thinking. I bet you'd love Shell Beach if you haven't been," he said. His eyes met hers, and he held her gaze as if offering a challenge. "Would you like to come with me tomorrow? I have to take some photographs for an article I'm writing, and I would love the company. The tide should be out, and the shells are everywhere. Special ones. You'd like it if you like shell hunting.

"Oh, I do. Very much. I haven't been in years. I'll have to check with Felicia, though. We had planned a workday tomorrow.

"Kyle's here. I'm sure she could do without you for a few hours. I'll pick you up at nine and I'll bring lunch. Just be ready.

"I'll check with Felicia…"

"Choose you. Choose happy. You'll have a great time. I promise. I already squared it with her tonight at dinner. She's fine. And I look forward to seeing you then."

She watched as he turned back toward his car and started whistling, his Hawaiian shirt billowing in the breeze.

Standing on the cliff as she watched his tail lights disappear down the beach, she wasn't sure whether to thank her friend or fault her for throwing her under the bus.

CHAPTER 13

$\mathcal{T}$he next morning, she woke up bright and early again. She hadn't expected to be doing anything that required decent clothes, and she rummaged through her duffel bag trying to pick out anything without wrinkles. It took a while, but she tugged on a black skirt that would be comfortable to walk in and laughed as she shrugged on a coral tank top. She'd worn a lot of black for the past several years, but since she'd already scared him with all the neon colors before, it might be good to get out of the black habit and she was glad she'd brought some things that were a little brighter. Happy to have a coral option, she threw the shirt over her head. Glancing in the mirror, she noticed that it brought out the blue of her eyes and smiled, noticing the sensation of excitement creeping in.

She quickly rubbed sunscreen over her arms and

legs and her favorite SPF30 moisturizer on her face. The sun was always so bright on the beach, and a sunburn was something she didn't need. Her fair skin usually burned, so she'd gotten in the habit of taking the extra precaution.

Quickly applying some mascara and chapstick, she grabbed her visor and a big bottle of water just as she heard a car honking outside the door. Sliding into her flip-flops, she closed the door behind her, wondering what kind of adventure this day might bring.

He stood by his shiny, white Range Rover, holding the door open with one hand and reaching toward her with the other.

"Your chariot awaits, milady," he said as he helped her up into the car.

"Oh, no," she groaned, laughing as she slid onto the tan leather.

"Too corny?" he asked, sliding in the driver's seat. "You said you love all things British. Just thought I'd lay it on thick."

Megan laughed as she rolled down the window, throwing a quick wave to Felicia and Kyle as they drove past toward the beach.

"Bring it on. I love it," she said, actually feeling the smile on her face reach inside to her heart.

The few miles flew by as the Range Rover ambled up the beach to their destination. The eclectic group of houses lining the shore ranged from trailers with shade covers to stucco boxes to virtual mansions made of the colorful ladrillo.

"That one looks like a castle," Megan remarked as they passed a house that looked like it should have been in Spain. Turrets and spiral columns surrounded a house that appeared to have at least ten bedrooms and an enclosed patio large enough for a restaurant.

"That's quite a house. It grows yearly, but never seems to have anyone in it. Just keeps getting mysteriously bigger," James said as they continued north.

"Slow down," Megan said suddenly, as something dark and big seemed to be moving up the beach in front of them.

The Ranger Rover slowed to a stop. "What do you see?" James said as he peered through the windshield.

"I can't tell what it is, but it's moving from the water toward the dunes." She couldn't quite make out what it was, and popped the door open to get a better look. She slowly moved toward the object, noticing that the beach was quiet, no other people in sight but James.

"Oh, it's a sea turtle! It's huge." she cried, her hand over her mouth. The turtle lumbered toward the high tide line, determined to reach its destination. "She must be heading up to lay her eggs. I've never seen that before."

"I've never seen it, either. I'm going to get my camera from the car," he said as he headed back to the Range Rover. "Just stay where you are," he called over his shoulder.

As Megan sat in the sand and watched the turtle begin to dig a hole to lay her eggs in, the warm breeze and silence overwhelmed her. She felt warm tears spill down her cheeks, overcome with gratitude to be able to witness such a thing. Her sadness melted as the turtle dug and rested her head on the sand, tired by her labor. She said a silent thank you, her eyes lifted to the sky, as she was gifted with such an amazing sight.

As she sat, mesmerized, she felt a warm hand on her shoulder. Turning, she met those eyes, the ones that were starting to melt her also. James gazed intently at her, his eyes clear and strong.

"What great good fortune to see this," he said. "I really don't know anyone who has down here."

Wiping her tears with her sleeve, she smiled up at him. "I don't, either, and I'm feeling quite blessed to be one who has," she said, turning her attention back to the turtle.

With a quick squeeze of her hand, James circled the turtle, careful to keep a respectable distance. The sound of the camera shutter floated on the breeze, and she marveled at the amazing scene.

He sat next to her again. They watched in silence as the turtle completed her task, the eggs deposited in the same place that the turtle itself had hatched. The whole experience had to have taken at least an hour, and in Megan's mind it had flown by in minutes. They both watched in silence, save for the periodic sound of the shutter of James's camera.

Eventually, the turtle rested her weary head on the side of the hole she'd dug, seeming to need the strength to get back to the water. Slowly, she lumbered out of the deep hole, her legs and arms pushing sand to cover her future offspring. As the sand reached the top, she slowly circled the hole, spreading the sand back and forth, leaving no evidence of the event that had just taken place.

Megan felt rooted to the spot, and as they watched, the turtle started the long trek back to the water. As she moved toward the waves, James moved over to the sand dune, the shutter of his camera clicking wildly. Resting a few times, the turtle met the water, the waves lapping at her nose. Slowly turning her head back toward her nest for one last look, her eyes turned back to the sea. Her head up and her neck strong, she moved toward the waves, moving forward with purpose into them. On the third wave, she floated, her renewed strength moving her arms and legs rhythmically. With the next wave, she was gone.

Megan realized that she hadn't moved, her arms wrapped around her knees tightly. Tears warmed her face once more, and she watched the turtle float in the waves and disappear. The sense of connection to nature swelled her heart, and the foreign feeling surprised her. For the first time in years, she realized that she had been completely engrossed, one hundred percent present in a moment that didn't involve humans. Not one shred of worry had crossed her mind, and she smiled, wishing that it could always be so. No worry, no anxiety.

"I think I got some really good shots," James said as he made a wide circle around where the turtle had laid her nest. "Look at this one."

On the camera screen that he held out to her as a perfect picture of the turtle's tracks moving toward the water, waves crashing beyond where they disappeared into the seas.

"That's beautiful," was all she could say as her tears dried, and her sniffles subsided. "That was over-whelming."

"It sure was." He popped the lens cover back on his camera. "Those are the kinds of things that time just must stop for. Not something you can pass up."

"I've never had the opportunity to stop before."

"There are lots of moments worthy of taking the time to experience. Most people choose not to."

She watched as he slung the camera over his shoulder, looking out to the horizon. "Do you see those pangas out there?" He pointed toward several of the typical Mexican fishing boats that regularly fished off shore.

"Barely. Maybe three of them?"

"Yes," he said. "Something's off about them. The Mexican panga boats don't fish in groups like that, at least not during the day. They've been out there for several days, and I've sent some pictures to my editor.

Maybe I got some good ones when they were closer, when the turtle was here."

"Is that part of the story you're writing?"

"No. Just not quite right," he said, his eyes still on the group of boats offshore. "Shall we continue on, milady?" He turned, extending his hand to her, pulling her up out of the sand. As they walked toward the car, he didn't let go of her hand, his squeezing hers. His calmness comforted her as she let him pull her along.

CHAPTER 14

*S*hell Beach loomed ahead as they continued on further up the coast. The beach flattened, widening out into a long spit reaching out to the sea, the shoreline covered with stones and shells. The houses faded away, and they climbed over the dunes to the spot he had in mind.

"Are you looking for something particular?" He had slowed down a bit, and seemed to be searching, his eyes scanning the beach.

"I drove up here the other day and found a great place with tons of sand dollars. I'm trying to spot it again." They crested a sand dune and he smiled, pointing to a place along the shore. "There it is.

Tossing her flip-flops in the car, Megan walked toward the water, the sand warming her toes and tickling at the same time. The water was warm, even, for this time of year, and as she stood with the waves lapping, she sighed, taking in the moment.

"Head out a little further, and you can feel them with your toes," James prompted, wading a little further out.

"The sand dollars?" Her eyebrows shot up, the memory of the crab hanging on her toe making her hesitate.

"Come on. Don't be afraid," he said, grabbing her hand and leading her further into the waves. "Sand dollars that are alive aren't in this close to the beach. They're out further, standing on end. It's the dead ones that wash up to shore, and they couldn't bite you anyway," he said, his eyes gleaming with laughter.

Feeling something hard between her toes, she bent down and grabbed a big sand dollar, rinsing it off in the water. "Look at this!" she cried, waving it in the air.

"Good one," he said as he held open a bag for her to put it in. They walked along the shore quietly, the bag filling quickly. In no time, they had a full bag.

"This is a good catch for one day." He held the bag open, and she realized it was more shells than she'd ever seen in one place.

"Are you sure we can take them?" she said, her eyebrows furrowing in concern. "We aren't breaking the rules?"

"Well, there are no laws against it. I think maybe the basic rule of things is don't take more than you need, and leave some for others," he said, his eyes now on the horizon again.

She wondered what he was looking for, thinking of all the rules that governed her existence. Do a good job, help people, make a difference. It all mattered to her.

James handed her the Mexican blanket he grabbed from the back of the car, and as she spread it out in the shade, she took in the bright colors and white fringe. Yellow, purple, red and green stripes covered the sand, and they sat as he opened the basket he'd brought along.

"So, all things British, huh?" he said, as he leaned into the basket. "We'll see about that." He chuckled as he brought out bread, a wedge of Stilton cheese, a jar of something brown and a big bottle of dark beer. "Ever had a plowman's lunch before?"

"I think I've read about it before in books set in England," she said as she picked up the brown concoction. "Branston Pickle? I know I've never heard of that before."

"Well, some things are just special. I can't get this here in Mexico. I've been saving it all for a special occasion." His eyes caught hers as he handed her a plate spread with cheese, bread and the chopped pickle. "Go on. Try it," he coaxed, suppressing a laugh as he cut up an apple and put it on her plate. "Just one bite. If you don't like it, you don't have to eat any more."

"Is it disgusting?" Her nose wrinkled as she bent

down to smell the brown stuff. It looked like jelly, but had chunks of something in it.

His laughter startled her, and she looked up to see his broad smile. "Well, I love it, but you may not. But how will you ever know if you don't try? Here. Put some of the pickle on the bread and top it with Stilton." He handed her a mug of dark beer. "Chase it with this if you have to."

She could feel him staring at her, and she was determined to take the challenge. She popped the bread in her mouth, her mouth tingling with the pleasant surprise.

"That's really good," she said, her mouth still full. She smiled with relief that it actually was good. She would have eaten it anyway so as not to disappoint him. That it was actually pleasing to her was a bonus.

They ate leisurely, the sound of the waves not breaking into their quick, easy conversation. Several times, James grabbed his camera, his artist's eye seeing something that she did not, and he fell into his creative work. He explained that he worked for Outdoor World, a travel magazine, and he was paid to write articles for them specifically about Baja.

"Fishing, mainly?" she asked, her interest piqued.

"Anything that travelers would want to know about. I've written about petroglyphs, fossil mounds, native Indians, food, art galleries. Anything that I find interesting that might be good for travelers. I even wrote an article about smuggling."

"What an exciting thing to do, to travel and share it with other people. I can't even imagine being so lucky."

As he put the camera down, he turned back to Megan and he smiled. "Why can't you be that lucky? Anybody can. You create your own luck."

She stopped and gazed at him thoughtfully. "That's not been my experience," she said. "I mean, I've tried to create my own luck. I suppose sometimes it just doesn't work out.

"Well, why not? What do you come to Baja for?

She thought for a moment, wondering how to explain her predicament. "I like coming down and not talking to a single human. Honestly, that's the appeal for me. I talk to people all day long at work and, mostly, they're unhappy. I like the quiet here."

"Unhappy? I don't think that sounds much fun. What could you do to make them—and you—happy?"

She was taken aback at his question. No one had ever posed it before, and she paused as she actually considered this. It was important to help teenagers and, while tough, extremely rewarding. But it had been a long time since it had been easy, and with money tight it was hard to find the fun in it.

"I run a home with my sister and brother-in-law for teenage girls who need help. I was a school principal before that, and I thought this was going to be different than it's turned out to be. Most of the girls are great—and grateful. But occasionally we're faced with problems bigger than we can solve."

"Ah, that explains a lot," he said, his eyes resting on hers for a brief moment before he turned toward the sea and smiled.

"What do you mean?" She'd barely met the man. What could that explain?

"I have to confess that I did see you at your friend's house, before we'd met. As you walked across the road, you were looking down and it seemed to me as if you had the weight of the world on your shoulders. It appears you have." He sat back on the blanket, his hand spinning the beer bottle in a circle thoughtfully.

"Well, I do have," she replied. Her mind immediately went to the ranch, her decision, the dream that wasn't coming true—for her, anyway. She continued to find solace in the fact that the majority of the girls who passed through their doors left in much better condition than when they'd arrived.

James broke the silence. "I guess we just have different philosophies in life, then," he said. "I believe that no one is responsible for all that happens, and that everything is going to be all right. Always."

"That's fine for you to say. You're retired, building your dream home, living in Baja on the sea. Not a care in the world."

"We obviously have much more to discuss. I have only just shared my philosophy, not my entire life history."

Her cheeks warmed at his comment, feeling as

though she'd overstepped and assumed that she knew more than she did. He was right.

"Well, tell me, then," she said, and patiently waited while he fell silent for a while.

"Ah, the life story part," he said with a smile. "I do hope we have more time to find out all that about each other, but suffice it to say that I have moved where my heart has pointed me my whole life. It hasn't been all roses, but I've managed to help along the way and met people from around the world. I am content. At the same time, I have created my own luck."

Megan scribbled in the sand with a stick of driftwood.

"What I meant to say is that I believe anyone can be happy as long as he or she chooses to be. And that it's your responsibility to be so. So, even if you started this business with a full heart and good intentions, there is no harm or failure in reconsidering. It's just a re-start."

She looked up from her hands into the eyes gazing at her. Startled at his intensity, he seemed to really mean it, sincerely believing that happiness was a choice.

"I don't understand how you can think that. I've got debt and partners and a commitment."

"A commitment to being miserable? Is that what you mean? Things ebb and flow in our lives. I can't believe that there aren't other people who could help the girls if you and your family decide to do something different. Help in a different way." He took her hand, pulling it toward him across the blanket. "I have seen many, many things that should make me miserable. I have been in situations that I never thought I could change. But I chose to make my life different. Chose to be happy. It is the one thing that you can and must do for yourself to ever live a complete life. Was it easy? Not always. But you can make choices that can make it right for everyone. Suffering forever isn't the best way to go."

"You make it sound so easy," she said, the ever-present knot of anxiety growing. "I can't let my partners down."

"You said that your partners are your sister and brother-in-law. Do you love them?"

"Oh, yes, very much. We're incredibly close, especially after these past few years working together."

"Do you believe they love you?"

"Absolutely. We would do anything each other."

"Everything but admit that you're all miserable, and release each other from the burden? Who's to say that there isn't someone waiting in the wings to help and very excited about it? And you can tackle the next challenge in your life. One that inspires you and uses your unique talents?"

His words stung, and the heat of his hand intensified her discomfort. She pulled back, standing up and stepping away from the blanket.

In a flash, Megan remembered the poignant conversation with her sister—where they'd both decided they actually weren't very happy, and maybe the girls would be better served in another environment. Maybe she actually should let herself think of other potential options.

"It's not like that. It's complicated."

"Megan, anything in life can be as easy or as complicated as you choose it to be. Choose happy."

Stepping away from the blanket, he walked toward the waves, his Hawaiian shirt flapping in the breeze. The blue fabric was covered in pictures of beer bottles, and written between the palm trees was, "It's five o'clock somewhere."

"Who couldn't be happy here? You'll see. Sink into your time here, and see what you find."

As she walked toward him to wiggle her feet in the water before they left, he turned, his hand brushing her cheek.

He had an uncanny way of making her forget about all of her problems—keeping the weight of the world at bay, even if just for a moment. She felt the breeze on her face, the sun on her skin. For a brief second, her mind cleared and all she knew was that in at least this moment, she was happy.

CHAPTER 15

*T*he whining of an engine jolted her back to reality and James abruptly pulled away, his hand shielding his eyes from the sun as he looked down the beach.

"Who is it?" she said, turning toward the sound of the truck as it approached.

"It's Manuel." His gaze followed the truck of their camp owner as it sped toward them, sliding to a stop in the sand behind the Range Rover.

The tall, slender Mexican man hopped from his truck and strode toward the shore, his long legs taking the distance quickly. His jeans neatly tucked into rubber fishing boots, Megan thought they looked much like the Wellies people wore in England to keep their feet dry. She remembered that the fishermen wore them while out on the pangas, probably to keep their feet free of hooks and fish guts, and knew Manuel spent a great deal of time fishing off the shore, amply feeding his family with enough to spare.

"Hola." He greeted them with a slight nod of his head, his black hair peeking out from beneath a San Diego Padres ball cap. He glanced from James to Megan, quickly grabbing his hat. As he looked at his feet, his fingers quickly worked the bill of the ball cap, twisting and untwisting it, his eyes never leaving the boats on the horizon.

With a nod of understanding to Manuel, James turned to Megan. "I think we need to talk in private. Do you mind waiting at the car for a moment," he asked?

With a smile and a nod to Megan, Manuel shifted from foot to foot, running his hands through his hair as Megan walked toward the car. As she slid into the seat, his voice rose above the sound of the waves as he fired off rapid Spanish, his arms gesturing wildly as he pointed toward the fishing boats offshore. Her Spanish was a little rusty, but she caught several words that she recognized and knew they were talking about the big fish, the totuaba, that Kyle had seen dotting the shore the previous day.

As James lifted the camera to his eye, he pointed it toward the horizon, scanning in the direction Manuel had pointed to. After several passes, he stopped, holding the camera steady. For several minutes, it seemed, he stood stock still, but she could hear the rapid sounds of the camera shutter from where she sat.

Manuel seemed satisfied as the camera was lowered, its cap replaced as James spoke slowly and so low that Megan couldn't hear what he was saying. Manuel held his hands out to James, palms up, as if asking for something. She saw James slowly shake his head, his eyes downcast.

Manuel's ball cap hit the sand as he threw it down on the ground. He slowly picked it up, pushed it hard on his head and turned toward his truck. In Spanish, James shouted something as the engine turned over in Manuel's truck. She thought she read disappointment in Manuel's eyes as he turned the truck south, speeding off toward the campo he came from.

James was silent as he approached the Range Rover, his frown something Megan had never seen before. Shoving the camera in its case, she could see the muscles in his jaw clench and his lips purse.

"What is it, James? What's happened?"

"I'm sorry, Megan. It's not something I can share with you. It's about an article I wrote a few months back." He quickly gathered the picnic remnants, roughly shoving the basket in the back of the car.

She peered at him with a sideways glance as he turned the car south and headed back home. *This doesn't exactly seem like 'happy',* she thought as his knuckles tightly gripped the steering wheel, his eyes straight ahead.

"Not another one," she heard him say, breaking the silence.

"What? That black fish?"

"Yeah. Another totuaba," he said as the car slowed to a stop. Without a word, he jumped from the driver's seat and grabbed his camera from the back.

Furiously snapping pictures around the large fish, he turned to her and said, "Can you grab that stick over there for me?"

Stick in hand, she stood by the fish and wondered what was happening. Its skin was lovely, sparkling in the sun, and it seemed to be whole. Maybe three feet in length, it would have been a great find for a hungry family.

Taking the stick, he placed it down toward the fish's belly, pulling up on the top of the fish. The movement exposed that the fish had been gutted before it was left on the beach, its innards gone.

"I need to take a picture of that. Can you hold it open?"

She hadn't had much fishing experience, and wasn't quite sure where to poke. He was completely focused on this fish, and she mustered up her courage, placing the stick inside the fish and lifting it open so he could photograph whatever it was he was looking for.

"Perfect. Can you hold it a little higher?" His shutter clicked away as he captured the fish from all angles.

"Like this?" She held the stick higher, exposing more of the fish.

"Yep, great. Thanks."

His lens cap back on the camera, he gently took the stick out of her hand, gazing at the fish lying on the shore. He turned slowly, looking back out to the horizon.

"What's happened to this totuaba?" she asked, crouching beside it. Nothing seemed wrong with it from its outside appearance, but now that she knew its insides had been taken, she wondered why that would be.

"I can't quite be sure, but I think that the smuggling has started up again."

"Smuggling? Here? Do you mean drugs?" She felt her hands clench.

"No, not drugs," he said, the corners of his mouth twitching into a smile. "So far, we've not had that problem around here, and I hope it stays that way."

"Well, what, then? Smuggling what?"

"A few months ago, I wrote an article about the totuaba in the area for the magazine. People had been accidentally catching them, and I had some good photographs of them. They're difficult to catch, as they usually stay really deep. They're not caught often."

"I thought I heard that they'd been over-fished and were endangered now. It's illegal to catch them?"

"You're right. Smuggling and sport fishing had decimated them, and they were designated as protected. It's illegal for Americans to catch them at all, but Mexican citizens can, in small numbers. And not commercially. Personal use only, to feed their families."

He circled the fish slowly as he talked. He seemed satisfied that he had enough pictures and put the camera back in the car.

"I still don't understand. What were people smuggling? The fish?"

"In my research for the article, I found that the bladder of this particular fish is used in a soup in Asia and is highly coveted."

"Soup?" She suppressed a laugh rising in her throat. It sounded absurd.

He caught her eye and grinned himself.

"I know it sounds ridiculous, but it's for a special fertility soup, dating back centuries. At today's prices, two hundred bladders from this fish would sell for almost three million dollars. Pretty big incentive, and they're only found here, in the northern half of the Gulf of California."

She gasped at the staggering amount of money. "You think someone's smuggling them now?"

"I'm not sure. I do know that it had a resurgence in popularity a couple decades ago, and people smuggled them out of the country and then on to Asia. It had stopped for a long time, and what I wrote about in the article was that it seemed that since the smuggling had stopped, the fish were making a comeback. Their numbers have increased in the last decade, and I was cheering that outcome."

"But by writing about it again, you reached a whole new audience with that information."

"That's what I was afraid would happen. I even asked my editor if it should be printed at all. I didn't want to give a whole new generation of criminals any ideas."

"So, you think that's what's happening now?" She wondered how anybody could do such a thing, waste so many lives of these fish and endanger them again.

"I'm not sure. I really didn't even want to mention it to you, but I suppose you earned the truth by holding a stick in a dead fish's gut," he said.

The smile had returned to his eyes, and she felt herself laugh.

"Well, I'm a helper, that's for sure. Always prepared to sacrifice myself for somebody else on a moment's notice." She wasn't kidding about that. It really did seem to be her purpose in life, no matter the cost to herself. This sacrifice didn't seem hopeless, though, as maybe she could help stop this from happening again.

They'd returned to the car now, and as they continued toward their campo she turned toward him, placing her hand gently on his arm.

"What do you plan to do?"

"I don't know yet. I notified my editor, for one. He'll need to know. He's the one that convinced me that it needed to be printed as is, including the information about the value to the overseas population in their efforts at fertility."

His chin set and his jaw hard, he squinted toward the horizon before he turned up into their campo.

Following his gaze, she saw several boats huddled together and wondered if they had anything to do with this slaughter they were witnessing. She shuddered to think that an entire species could be wiped out for soup.

CHAPTER 16

*A*s they pulled into their campo, James's grip on the steering wheel loosened and his eyes softened. He turned in to her driveway, the sand crunching under the tires of the Range Rover.

He quickly hopped out, opening her door before she even had a chance to gather her things. He grabbed the bag of shells they had collected and walked in behind her as she opened the door.

"These shells are spectacular," he said, laying them out on her counter. "I've never seen some of these before. This one has to be a paper nautilus—actually an octopus egg container."

As he pulled the shells out of the bag, she watched as he set them down in a mosaic pattern, almost like a mandala. A huge clamshell lay in the middle, and he quickly placed the other assorted shells around it in a pattern that looked, to her, like rays of the sun.

"That's beautiful. How do you do that?" she asked, peering over his shoulder.

He shrugged as he continued to place the shells in a beautiful pattern. "Just like the painting we did. You just check in about how they make you feel, and ask what to do next."

"You make it sound so simple. The blue tulips were really tough for me to do."

"But you did it," he said, winking at her.

She peered over at her wood stove and had an idea.

"I've always wanted to add something like that on the hearth over there by the wood stove. The ashes fall out onto the carpet, so I wanted to do something creative, but I'm afraid to."

"There you go again. Afraid of what?"

"I don't know. Doing it wrong?"

"There is no wrong. Didn't we prove that with the blue tulips?" He smiled, turning toward her. She couldn't read his sentiment as he took her hand and placed it on his cheek. He gazed into her eyes as his danced with mischief.

"I have an idea. I'll be right back," he said as he headed out the door.

Within minutes, he was back with a bucket, a trowel and a bag of some kind of powder.

"We're going to do your hearth right now."

"Right now? I can't. I'm not ready."

"When will you be ready?" he asked, standing in

front of her. His blue eyes never left hers, the challenge clear.

"Um, maybe next week?"

"How about never, if you had your way. We're going to do it now."

She felt the sweat on her palms as he filled the bucket with the sand-colored powder and water, mixing it quickly with the trowel.

"You'd better get your ideas sorted out. The grout will dry if we leave it too long." She quickly turned to the shells, and panic rose in her chest.

"I'll just do the pattern you did. It's pretty."

He set the bucket down, turning to the counter. In one swift motion, he rearranged all of the shells, obliterating the pattern he had made.

His blue eyes bore into her as he leaned on the counter with one elbow. "What are you going to do now?"

"I–I don't know. I don't know how to do this. I don't want to mess it up."

"That's not possible. It will be your creation, and it will be perfect, whatever it is," he said, picking up the bucket and heading toward the cement hearth. "I'm spreading the grout now, so you have about ten minutes to decide what you want to do."

Her hands now completely drenched and her heart fluttering, she quickly sorted the shells on the counter, arranging and re-arranging them in different patterns.

She shook her head, moving them all around again, not satisfied with her effort.

"One-minute warning," she heard from the corner of the room.

Panicked, she gathered the shells she had chosen and rushed to the wood stove. She looked at him, laughing. "Please don't make me do this. I can't. I'll ruin it. I'm not creative."

He set the trowel in the bucket, pointing to the grout he had spread on the cement square in front of the wood stove.

Taking her hand, he pulled her down toward the floor. They sat in front of the blank canvas of grout, her shells piled by her side.

"There is nothing you can do that would be wrong. This is your house. It will be your creation, your memory of gathering shells today on the beach. Close your eyes, take a deep breath, and create."

His eyes intent, she turned her gaze toward the floor. Taking the shells in her hand, she closed her eyes for a moment, breathing deeply and vowing to let the shells fall where they should.

As she placed the big shell in the center and pushed it into the grout, she turned to see him gazing, his lips turned up in a smile. He moved back a bit, encouraging her to continue.

"Go on. You can do it."

Smiling, she turned back to the hearth. She felt a joy come over her as she picked up shells of purple, gold, and green. Matching stones fell into place swiftly by her hand, and she felt as if time stopped as she placed them where she felt they needed to be.

She reached for another shell and, almost in a daze, she realized she was out of shells. She suddenly stood, taking a step back and bumping into him standing behind her. She felt his arms around her waist, his cheek next to hers as he looked down at what she had created.

"Look at what you've done," he said, rubbing his beard against her cheek, grabbing her more tightly. "It really is beautiful."

Her heart swelled as she looked at the mandala she'd created with the gifts from the sea. She was stunned that she'd done it. *Is this what it feels like? Happy?* she thought? If it was, she wanted more of it.

He pulled her around to face him, holding her tightly to him. She lowered her head on his shoulder, feeling his heart beat. Closing her eyes, she felt her heart opening, her creation still fresh in her mind. He stepped back, his hand on her chin, tilting her face up toward his.

"You have so much inside that you've never known," he said as he lowered his lips to hers.

The sound of a car horn blasted the silence, and she stepped back, startled. It wasn't a sound common here at the beach. Whoever was honking was really laying it on, the horn blaring wildly. The blasts were coming from the direction of James's house, and he looked out the door to see who it was.

His eyes narrowed as he peered down the road. With a look of concern, he turned back toward her. "I'll be right back. I'll grab my camera while I'm over there and we'll memorialize your art work," he said, squeezing her hand before he walked out the door.

CHAPTER 17

She studied her handiwork for a bit, marveling at how she'd gotten the shells in just the right places. It really was pretty, if she did say so herself, and she laughed at the thought that she'd actually had the courage to do it.

She hummed as she cleaned the tools he had brought, washing the grout off of the trowel with warm water. She'd cleaned the bucket, too, by the time she realized he hadn't returned. Drying them off with a towel, she headed out the door to return them.

She passed a police car in the driveway and wondered if this had been the car that had been honking so loudly. She started up the colorful tile steps toward his house, anxious to see him.

The front door was open, and she stopped in her tracks as she heard loud voices arguing. Worried she might get caught eavesdropping, she turned to leave, but felt herself drawn to stay, as the voices grew louder.

"Senor, we have no other evidence right now to stop these smugglers. Your pictures are the only way to get a warrant quickly. We need them."

"You have no way to take pictures yourselves? This is not something I want to get involved in. I told Manuel that."

Manuel's voice broke into the exchange. "Don't you understand? We live here. This is our home. And it's your home now, too."

"Yes, it is my home, but I don't want to get involved. My editor has told me not to. I could lose my job."

Manuel's voice sounded tired. "Fishing is too important to the people here, to their livelihood. There aren't enough totuaba to supply them to other countries."

"I didn't ask you to come here. I took the pictures only to tell you what I suspected." Anger seeped into James's voice as he continued. "I actually don't want to get involved with any of this."

The scrape of chairs sounded as the men abruptly stood up.

"Senor, we need those pictures."

"You don't know what you're asking me to do," James said, his voice low.

"Please reconsider, Senor. We need your help."

James was silent as she heard the men heading toward the door.

She felt the heat rise in her cheeks as her face flushed with panic. She heard the men heading toward the door, and tried to find a place to hide before they saw her. Setting the bucket of tools down as quietly as she could, she turned and jumped around the corner of the house, out of sight from the front door.

The men stomped down the stairs, the policeman's face red, fists clenching as he strode toward the police truck. She ducked further behind the house as they hopped into the car and sped off, sand shooting from the spinning tires.

She wrestled with whether or not to go inside and talk to James—how could this be true, that he wouldn't help—but just as she started up the steps, she heard his voice again.

"No, I won't do that. No, I'm not interested. I intend to stay completely out of it."

She had no idea who he was talking to, but it was clear that he wasn't going to stand up for what was right. He wasn't going to do right thing, fight for the underdog. And if that was the case, she didn't want to have anything to do with him.

CHAPTER 18

*T*ears stung her cheeks as she ran down the road, her head fighting her heart. As she neared her house, she started up toward Felicia's, her thoughts jumbled and confused. The light shone from Felicia's house and she heard laughter coming from the windows, something she had no interest in. She turned back toward the cliff and to her own safe haven. As she pushed the door of her house open, she stumbled inside.

She'd set the wood stove up with logs before she'd done the hearth today, and she struck a match quickly, the logs lighting on the first try. The door of the stove hung open, the light of the flames dancing on the shells she had carefully placed earlier.

She closed the door of the stove and twisted down the metal handle, flames still glowing through the clear glass onto the shells.

"What happened?" she heard, as her door opened and Felicia walked in. She set a bottle of wine on the counter, grabbed a corkscrew and deftly opened the bottle. "I saw you run out of James's house but couldn't catch you before you came back here. Have you been crying?"

Taking the glass of wine that Felicia held out to her, she walked over to the wood stove, plopping down on the sofa.

Felicia followed, her eyes glued on the hearth.

"Where did that come from? That wasn't there last night."

Megan regained her composure as she looked at the beautiful array of shells that James had coaxed out of her earlier.

"I thought...I thought..." she said slowly before she decided not to continue. She'd only had a brief glimpse into a man who had shown her parts of herself that she hadn't known existed—that he wasn't everything she'd thought he was shouldn't really be a surprise. She'd met so many troubled people in her time helping—it actually shouldn't be a surprise at all.

"Thought what?" her friend said, settling in beside her on the couch. "What did he do? Do I need to go poke him in the eye?"

Megan smiled in spite of herself, pushing Felicia's shoulder.

"No, friend. But I might do it myself."

She recounted the events of the day, from the sea turtle laying its eggs to the totuaba to the new hearth.

"It was all going so well. I've never had a day quite like today."

"Sounds good so far. The hearth is gorgeous. I never knew you had it in you," she said, smiling as she poured more wine into Megan's glass.

"Well, that was the good part of what happened. Did you hear all that honking earlier?"

"Yeah, we saw a police car pull up at James's, and they were laying on the horn."

"Well, that guy was arguing with him when I went to take back his tools later."

"What about?"

"You're not going to believe this. He knows about the smuggling. You know the totuaba that Kyle found on the beach? Somebody's killing them and smuggling their bladders overseas. I think he's involved.

"Excuse me? After a day like today, the turtle and everything? What a jerk."

"I really felt like we were on the same page. He seemed so content, so happy. And carefree."

"Well, you can be pretty carefree if you're making the kind of money those would get you. Are you sure?"

"I'm almost positive. The policeman in the house was talking about the pictures and asked for them, but James refused."

Felicia gazed at the fire, deep in thought. "He

seemed to me to be more like you, concerned about people and protecting the campos."

"That's what I thought. I don't know what happened. How could I have been so wrong?"

"Oh, honey, don't worry about it. Come over to my place. We're making clams."

"You?" Megan's eyebrows shot up at the surprise of Felicia cooking anything.

"Well, not me. Kyle. But you need to come over and be with friends. If he's involved in that, he's no friend of ours. Honestly, he doesn't deserve you. You're the nicest person I've ever met. It's honestly annoying sometimes. You make me look bad."

Megan laughed. There was no question she'd spent her life helping people, and it was almost as if she had to. It meant a lot to her, and anyone that she was going to spend time with would see the value—feel the same —and help when they could. "I guess we don't see eye to eye. No harm, no foul. I learned some things about myself, anyway. I can actually be creative," she said, gesturing to the hearth and her painting. "So it wasn't a total loss."

"If he can't see the big heart you have, it's *his* loss. And if he's capable of something like that, you can't be with him anyway. You're the kindest, most compassionate person I know. Not to mention, a ridiculous rule-follower. You could never be with a smuggler."

"I just can't believe he is one. Not after today, not after seeing him so upset at the dead fish. And excited about the sea turtle laying her eggs." Her head fell into her hands now, her shoulders slumped.

"What are you going to do?"

"I'm not sure. We can't let them cover up a smuggling ring, can we? Shouldn't we do something?"

"Not tonight, that's for sure. Come on. Let's eat lots of clams with butter, and finish this wine. Things will look better tomorrow. Heck with him. Like I said, he doesn't deserve you."

"Felicia, I know you're trying to make me feel better. I'm just confused. I don't understand what's going on."

"Well, come be confused over at my place. We can play Scrabble. If you're that confused, maybe I can win for once. I promise I won't cheat," she said, as she grabbed the bottle and pulled Megan out the door. They made the short trip across the road and Megan waved at Kyle as he stood at the stove.

"Kyle steamed the clams since we couldn't find you. The butter should be ready, too," her friend said as she set plates out on the patio table. They'd sat on the porch overlooking the waves, enjoying the sweet gifts from the sea as the wine disappeared from their glasses.

Megan tried to focus as thoughts of James and the police rushed back in at every turn. Felicia rarely won at Scrabble when they played, but tonight had been different.

"Wow, you really are out of it," Felicia said as she

played her last tile, winning the second game in a row. "I never win at this."

Megan turned to her friend, trying to focus her eyes and willing the fog in her brain to lift.

"I don't' know what's the matter with me." Her head dropped to her hands, and she felt her friend's hand on her shoulder.

"Well, I do. You've been so focused on helping other people for such a long time, you've forgotten you have your own needs to tend to. You've opened your heart for the first time in a long time. I'm so sorry it got stepped on. But please don't let it stop you from keeping it open. I've missed this part of you," she said, her hand squeezing her friend's. "You'll feel better tomorrow. Get some sleep tonight, and we'll go let the air out of his tires in the morning when he's not looking."

CHAPTER 19

*W*ith a hug from her friend, she headed over to her house and tossed a few more logs on the fire. As she sat before the wood stove, the beautiful shells on the hearth caught her eye. The joy she'd felt when she'd laid them carefully on the hearth, her fear conquered and her heart light with his challenge and encouragement, felt fresh again.

From the corner of her eye, she saw a black bundle of fur scratching at the door.

"Whiskers!" she said, as she opened the door to let the dog in. His tail wagged at full speed as he ran in circles at her feet, and she knelt to pet him, her head peering past him as she waited for Jimmy's inevitable arrival.

"Hey," she heard him growl as he rounded the corner. He never was one for elaborate greetings.

"What's the matter? You don't look great." He sat

down beside her and opened the wood stove. Poking the coals, he added another log.

Comforted by his presence, and laughing at his blunt observation, she told him what she had heard from James.

"The Federales? The Mexican police?"

"That's right." She rested her hand on Whiskers' head, slowly shaking her own.

Jimmy laughed. "So James said no?"

"Yes, and they didn't seem very happy with that answer. Why wouldn't he help?"

"Can't explain that. James's an interesting character. He has a good sense of right and wrong, and really cares about Baja. But he's been around the block a few times. Sometimes being happy means minding your own business."

"But something as big as smuggling, right here in our front yard? How could you ever look the other way for that?" Her eyes misted at the thought of the fish disappearing forever, and she felt her anger rise at the thought that James might not do anything about it, might not follow the rules.

Jimmy leaned back a bit and peered at Megan. "You sound just like Cassie and the vaquita. She comes by it honestly, I'll say."

Megan sighed. Her daughter had been passionate about saving the vaquita for years and years, and her commitment had grown into the sanctuary. And Megan had taught her at a very young age that they had a responsibility to help when they could. So Jimmy was right—this was no different for her than the vaquita were for Cassie.

Jimmy cleared his throat, bringing her back to the present. "But I did talk with James this afternoon, and there's something I want to tell you."

"You did?" Confused, she looked up at her friend.

"Yep. I don't usually get involved in this kind of stuff, either."

"What is it with you guys not wanting to get involved? How can you ever feel good about yourself without helping other people?"

"Well, that's why I'm here. I'm trying to help. I've never seen him quite like this before. All he talked about was you."

Megan lost her breath for a moment. "He did? I don't understand that. We've barely met, and clearly we're not of the same mind in lots of areas."

"I don't think that's true. Maybe you two ought to clear that up." He took her hand, pulling her into a hug. "Life's too short not to be happy."

"What is it with all this 'be happy' stuff?" she said, not able to suppress a laugh.

"I don't know. Just decide what happy looks like for you, and make it happen," he said, heading out the door, Whiskers following behind.

CHAPTER 20

*J*immy had gone a while ago, and she found herself sitting on the cliff, staring at the water. The sound of her phone ringing jolted her back into the present. She read the display, letting out a deep sigh as she pulled herself back into reality.

"Hello, dear sister. How are you?"

"I'm good. Just wanted to make sure you were all right. And give you a bit of news," Annie said. "You okay?"

She didn't have the energy to share with her sister what had happened the past few days. "Yes, I'm good. It's beautiful here."

"Ah, it always is. I hope you're enjoying it. And I think you might enjoy it a little more now."

"What? I've been spending most of my time trying

to figure out what to do about the ranch. We've got to make a decision soon."

"Well, it's going to be a different kind of decision." She sounded like a kid at Christmas, waiting to open presents.

"What the heck? Spill."

"I don't quite know how to say this. I'm still spinning. Daniel and I are just shocked."

"You've got to put me out of my misery." Her hands tightened around the phone as she prepared herself for anything. The past few years had been tough, and she was used to getting bad news. "Just get it over with and tell me."

"Do you remember the award we won for best rehab facility from the state?

"Yes. It was one of the rare highlights in the past few years."

"Well, somehow we got noticed by a corporation that runs horse ranches like ours all over the country. They want to buy the business and bring it into their fold."

Her breath rushed out of her as she sat down hard on the chair outside, overlooking the ocean.

"Are you joking?"

"No, I'm not. It's an amazing offer, too. Enough to pay off all the debt and then some. Quite a bit more than that."

"Oh, my gosh. I'd never thought that going private rather than relying on public funds might make a difference. Is that something that we should consider on our own? To make a go of it with different funding?"

The line went silent for a bit, and Megan wondered if the call had been dropped. Finally, her sister spoke.

"Megan, income or no income, we talked about this. Remember when we were waiting for Eliana at the airport and we sat on the bench and asked each other if we were really happy? And we decided we weren't. That hasn't changed. This is a way to move on, find other ways to help and let the girls still be in good hands. Just not in our hands."

Megan took a breath and considered what her sister had said, and she knew she was right.

"And I will add—you sound completely different. I don't know if things are going well or not for you, but there's a different tone in your voice. You sound —lighter."

After sharing a few more particulars, they'd agreed to talk again in a few days while they all three considered their options.

Her head spinning with the new information, she watched the last sunlight disappear behind her, the horizon of the ocean turning to a lovely shade of lavender. The light changed once more, and she watched as the horizon disappeared altogether, the sky and the water the same color for that brief moment that she looked forward to every day.

The beauty of the water overwhelmed her, and she

gave in to the rush of emotion she had kept at bay until now. Relief enveloped her, all of the anxiety that had been ever-present with the girls' home evaporating with the news she had just gotten. She had thought her path was clear, continued sacrifice laid out before her. No retirement, no savings—no happy.

Now, with everything different, she would be free to choose her own path, and find her own happiness. Her breath hitched in her throat and her emotions overtook her, and overwhelmed with both joy and sorrow, she watched the last light of the day disappear.

As darkness fell, she walked inside toward the glow of the wood stove, placing another log in. The fire grew, warming the house and it seemed like the perfect time to grab a warm bath. She set candles all around the blue marble bathtub, determined to let the bubbles wash away the pain she was feeling. Even with the good news about the ranch, her heart was heavy about James. Pinning her hair on top of her head, she dropped her clothes on the floor and sunk into the hot water, hoping it would warm her heart.

She refused to think about James as she relaxed, taking in the beautiful blue marble of the tub and the colorful bricks that surrounded her, her mind settling on the lovely couple she had bought the house from. They had built it with love, just for the two of them, and had hired a special builder to help them. She smiled a bit at the thought that it wasn't until recently that she'd met the man who'd built it, and it turned out that her daughter was marrying his nephew. It was such a small world, and she'd enjoyed meeting Pablo when she'd come out for the vaquita sanctuary groundbreaking. She supposed she'd be seeing Pablo at the wedding, and that made her heart lighter.

He had only built churches before, and the love and pride he'd put into those buildings had been placed here in her home, as well. He had taken his time with this home, lovingly matching the patterns in the ladrillo so that all of the bricks were placed just so.

The first owners had been married for fifty years, and the house was designed to be a cozy place, just for two. They'd decided to use saloon doors from the house into the bathroom, creating an atmosphere of intimacy. She'd considered changing them out for a door with a lock, but had decided there wasn't any reason to as she was usually there alone.

Now, as the doors swung open, she gasped, sinking as far as she could into the bubbles in the tub.

"What are you doing here? You can't just keep letting yourself in places like that." Her eyes darted around the room as she tried to locate a towel or a robe, anything she could throw over herself that was within arm's reach. As she searched for a towel, she sighed as she realized there weren't any she could reach and she was grateful that she'd put in enough bubble bath that there wasn't anything exposed.

James stood in the doorway, running his hands through his hair.

"I thought I'd have a better chance of you not running away again if you were...incapacitated."

"Well, I sure am that. If I could, I'd throw you out right now." She sunk deeper into the tub and looked away. "I really have nothing to say to you. You need to leave."

"Megan, you've got to hear me out. It's not what it seemed." He sat on the side of the tub, placing his hand lightly on her chin. He pulled her face toward his and waited until she looked up at him.

"I don't want to hear anything you have to say."

"I can see you're going to make me do this the hard way. I won't leave until you hear me out. Please, Megan. I need to explain things to you. I'll wait for you by the fire. "

She shook her head, wrapped the towel around her and stepped out of the tub. She wasn't sure what to think. Why was he here now? What would she say?

She shrugged her robe over her shoulders and found her slippers, easing her feet into them as she headed out to the fire. As she rounded the corner, she stopped short. James was on the couch, his elbows on his knees as he stared into the flames. She sat beside him, waiting for him to speak.

"I wanted to explain what you overheard, but you left too quickly."

"I was just in shock, I think. I thought...I guess I thought you were different. When I heard you were involved with the smuggling, I just didn't know what to do. You keep telling me to be happy. But in my world, smuggling could never make me happy."

"What makes you think I am involved in the smuggling?" He rubbed the back of his neck, pacing back and forth in front of the hearth. "I've never been a smuggler and don't plan to become one now."

"I thought that's what you were talking about with the police."

"As you probably heard, they asked for the pictures that I took yesterday. They believe they are the smugglers and need the pictures for evidence." His eyes drilled into hers as he sat down again next to her.

"I heard that. I can't believe you won't help."

"I can't. I heard from my editor, and he's forbidden me to give them to anyone. He said he spoke with the magazine's attorneys, and the magazine doesn't want to get involved."

"Your editor said that? How could they do that? I thought your editor supported your story?"

"Yes, that's the confusing thing. He's the one I told you about who wanted me to print the story a few months back about the totuaba and the smuggling. Even what they did with the bladders."

"If he wanted you to do it then, why doesn't he want you to write about the fact that it's happening again?"

"I don't know. I can't quite piece it together, but he's forbidden me from writing the story. I sent him pictures of the smugglers that I found in my shots from yesterday. Said he owned the pictures since I submitted and I'd lose my job if I did."

"That doesn't make any sense. You've already written about it once before. What's the difference now?"

"I don't know," he said, standing again. He didn't seem to be able to stay in one place for long. The man standing before her now was certainly not the one she'd come to know. His agitation was new to her.

"What are you going to do?" Her blue eyes searched his.

"If I write the story or give up the pictures to the police, I'll get fired. This isn't something I chose to get involved in."

She stood herself, moving toward him. Her eyes met his, and she took his hand.

"James, I can't believe that being happy means not caring about things, not getting involved. Not following rules is one thing, but not being responsible and doing what's right is something else completely."

"The happiness of the entire world is not my responsibility. You seem to think it's yours, but that's not the way I operate. This is likely something better left alone. It could be dangerous, and I like living here."

"If you don't do something, nothing will change. The fish will be gone in no time."

"Taking responsibility for all things, taking care of others at your own expense is not the only right way to be." He pulled away from her and leaned against the kitchen counter.

"I think there's a place in the middle, where you can take care of yourself and balance that with how much you do for others. But ignoring what's right? I can't respect that."

He looked at her quizzically, his arms folded over his chest. She swallowed hard as his eyes held hers, and she tightened her robe around her. In one step, he was next to her, gathering her in his arms. She rested her head on his shoulder and felt his beard against her cheek, his scent comforting. She felt the wetness of her tears on his shirt as his arms squeezed around her.

"I think I should go. It's late, and I have some thinking to do." He released her, gently placing his hand on her chin. "Thank you for sharing your softer world with me, Megan. Maybe there is something in the middle." With a soft kiss to her forehead, he turned and walked out the door.

CHAPTER 21

*M*egan woke with a start as she heard cars roaring down the dirt road to the beach. The sun peeked over the horizon as dawn broke over the sea. It was early for so much noise and she hopped out of bed, hopping on one leg as she pulled her sweats on over her pajamas. Tugging on her Uggs, she grabbed her sunglasses and headed outside.

Felicia stood across the road, coffee in hand and motioned for Megan to come over, holding up her cup of coffee. A horn blared as she started to cross, and she stepped back off the road. She held up her hands in mock surrender as at least four trucks sped by, all pulling fishing boats. There were small boats with single motors and larger ones, all types and sizes and varying states of disrepair, all making a beeline for the beach. As the last one passed, she looked both ways and ran across to where Felicia was standing.

"What's that all about? Is it a parade or something?" Megan looked after the boats, her mouth open.

"I have no idea. All I know is that James knocked on the door before the sun came up and asked for Kyle. They stood outside talking for a while, then Kyle grabbed his stuff and left."

"He didn't say where he was going?"

"He just said he had to take care of something important. That's all I know. Have you talked to James?"

"He came over last night, and I guess there's something going on with the smugglers. He didn't want to get involved, and I told him I couldn't respect that decision."

"That sounds about right. What if they get in trouble?" Felicia held out a cup of coffee to her friend. "Did you think about that?"

Megan poured French vanilla creamer in her coffee. It was the only way she could get it down. "No, I don't think I suggested anything crazy. Where do you think they're going?"

Felicia grabbed her jeans and changed out of her pajamas. Pouring coffee into a travel mug, she grabbed her jacket. "No clue. But I know how to find out."

They stood on the roof of Megan's house and looked for a level spot to place the telescope that Felicia had brought over.

"I haven't used this thing in ages. Hope it still works." She pulled open the legs on the tripod. "We should be able to see exactly what they're doing with this thing. If it can see the moon, it can see where those boats went."

Megan grabbed the telescope from the case, carefully taking off the lens cap. As she set it on the tripod, Felicia tightened the bolts and turned some dials.

"I think it's just like a big pair of binoculars, isn't it?" She scanned the horizon, back and forth, finally settling on one spot. "There they are!"

"What? Where?" Megan certainly hoped that it was the makeshift flotilla, and hoped that they weren't doing anything too dangerous. It had never occurred to her when she had shared her feelings about being responsible that it might lead to an event like this.

"They're out there, all the boats. It looks like they're just floating. That's weird." She stood back, gesturing for Megan to take a look.

As she peered through the telescope, she saw a large circle of boats, some that she had not long ago seen hurrying down the road. In the center were three pangas, the same that had been on the water the day before. It was those pangas that James had been focused on with the lens of his camera.

Now, she saw him talking to one of the men on the panga.

"Felicia, Kyle's out there, too. I think they've surrounded the smugglers."

"No. No way. That's..." Her voice trailed off as she took a turn at the telescope. "Well, look at that. Who are all those guys with James? Where did all those boats come from?"

"I have no idea," Megan said as she held her hand over her eyes, squinting to try to see what was happening.

"Um, this is like a TV show. You're not going to believe this one. Gosh, I hope they don't have guns."

"Nobody has guns down here but the police," Megan reminded her. "That would get you in more trouble than you'd know how to get out of. Remember when Jimmy went to jail because they found those guns his dad had left after he retired as a sheriff?"

"I forgot about that. Maybe the smugglers are smart enough to know that, too. I hope so."

Megan stood back from the telescope, her eyes wide. "Look at that."

They both stood up as three large, black boats came from the south, speeding toward the group of boats out on the water.

"I hope those aren't reinforcements for the smugglers."

Felicia bent to look into the telescope. She let out a gasp as she peered at the scene.

"It's the Mexican Navy," she said, her hand on top of her head. "This is surreal."

They watched as the Navy boats surrounded the smaller fishing vessels, taking the smugglers on board and towing the pangas behind them as they headed south again. As the marine cavalry headed toward shore, they packed up the telescope.

"I am dying to find out what happened. Let's go meet them on the beach." Megan hurried down the stairs, Felicia right behind her as they grabbed the quads and headed out.

Their quad engines hummed as they headed toward the part of the beach that the boats had launched from. The trucks and trailers were parked along the cliff, and they hopped off the quads and headed toward the shoreline. Russell ran along behind, barking all the way.

As the boats pulled in, Megan spotted Kyle and James in the lead boat. Kyle was piloting the boat, and they were deep in conversation. As they neared the shore, James stood as he spotted Megan on shore. The instant the boat had run up on the sand, he hopped out and covered the distance between them in long strides.

He gathered her up in his arms, and she hugged him tightly.

"I can't believe what you just did," she said, as she caught her breath. He smelled like sea spray, and she never wanted to let him go.

"How do you know what I just did?" he asked as he looked from Megan to Felicia.

"Um—" Felicia started, and Megan shook her head and waved her off.

"I don't know if I was supposed to or not, but we got out the telescope and spied on you guys."

"Right. We did that," Felicia said.

"And we're really glad we did, because it was a sight to behold," Megan said. "I really still can't believe you just did that."

"I couldn't have done it without the south campos cavalry," he said, with a laugh. They turned and watched all the other boats as they beached. There were at least ten, and among them she recognized Jimmy and Manuel, the camp owner. As the men hopped out of the boats, there was much backslapping and high-fives all around.

Felicia ran over to Kyle, wrapping him in a bear hug.

"Come on, Mom, stop." He started to push her away, but she wouldn't let go. He gave in and hugged her back, rolling his eyes at James.

"You were all so brave," Megan said as the commotion died down. "I sure admire what you did," she said, her eyes directed at James.

"Let's get the boats out of the water, and have breakfast at my house, guys." James grinned from ear to ear. "I'll tell you all about it back at the house," he said, squeezing Megan's hand.

CHAPTER 22

Felicia and Megan hopped up onto the quads, taking the beach trail back up to the house. As they rounded the corner, Megan stopped short, Felicia almost running into her from behind.

"What was that for?" Felicia said. "You almost knocked Russell off."

The dog's eyes were wide as he tried to grip the seat of the quad and not slide off into the sand.

"A red SUV is at James's house And there's a man poking around." She cut the motor of the quad as she looked further up the road. "There's something shady. Look at that guy walking around and looking in the windows. There's something off about him."

"The guys are going to take a little while. We can't just sit here."

"Can you see him? He's watching the boats load up through binoculars. Look. He's out on the cliff."

The man slowly lowered the binoculars as he looked toward the boats on the shoreline packing up to head toward land. Suddenly, the binoculars clattered to the ground. He turned and ran toward his car along the side of the house.

"Okay, that's not normal," Felicia agreed as they watched him jump into the SUV, the engine turning over immediately.

"We need to follow him and find out what he was doing there." Megan started her quad and signaled for Felicia to follow her.

"What? Are you nuts? I can't. I only have enough gas to get back to the house. And you shouldn't go, either."

"I have to. I think he might have something to do with this."

Felicia's eyes darted from the boats on the beach to the SUV and settled on the dust coming from tires as Megan chased off after the red SUV.

"Okay, Russell. Let's hope there's nothing going on," Felicia mumbled as the dust plumes rose from the road.

CHAPTER 23

*M*egan drove the quad slowly behind the SUV as it tore down the access road toward the highway. Her heart thumped wildly as she wondered what she was getting herself into. She knew the man wouldn't recognize her, had never seen her, but she didn't want to draw his attention. Just the thought of what she was doing was making her hands sweat already, even though she knew it was the right thing to do.

The car turned south on the main road toward the small town that served the south campos. The SUV didn't slow as it neared the village, passing by the hardware store sandwiched between the two local restaurants, passing the small school for the local children and turning into the lot in front of the market, dirt flying.

One of the large restaurant signs gave good camouflage as she stopped and pulled out her phone, pretending to make a call and looking quickly in the other direction. Her hands fumbled with the phone as she pretended to dial, accidentally hitting the contact for "Mom."

Quickly pushing "end call", she pretended to talk on the phone. That wouldn't raise suspicion in the poblado, as the phone service off the road was spotty at best for most people, and this parking lot served as a makeshift phone booth for people to call the U.S.

As the man stood outside the market, she slowly pulled up to the side of the building, quietly turning off the quad and hopped off, her back against the side wall. Inching slowly, she got close to the window and strained to hear the voices inside that were growing louder.

She turned to look into the window, peeking just her head over the sill to see who was inside speaking. As she tried to keep her face low enough not to be seen, the tall man from the SUV poked his finger into the chest of another man, one that Megan did recognize.

The shorter man tried to back away, his hands held up in surrender. The man's anger was rising along with his voice, his red cheeks puffed and spittle flying as he continued to yell at the shorter man.

The muffled argument was getting louder, but she couldn't quite make out any words besides totuaba. She crouched down toward the ground. *I should just get out of here,* she thought, her muscles tense. She couldn't bring herself to leave. If she left, no one would know that the man was involved with this somehow. James would never know.

Megan's hand inched upward to slide the window open to hear what they were saying. She swallowed hard and pushed, opening the window a crack.

"I got the camera. I've destroyed the data card. There's nothing to connect me to the smuggling now, but the other guys have been caught." The man paced in the market, oblivious to the other customers who had fallen silent.

"You must have told him about my plans." He stopped pacing, his finger in Manuel's chest. "I told you if you got James involved, you'd be sorry."

"I didn't tell him anything, Senor. I swear."

"You did tell him. You had to. Why else would he be out on the water acting like John Wayne and the cavalry?" His eyes bulged and his hands flailed wildly in the air.

"Senor, you must believe me. I have kept your plans to myself and told no one," Manuel stammered.

The man appeared to be considering what Manuel had said, and turned to look at the shocked customers standing still, watching the exchange. Blinking hard at the people in the market staring at him, he grabbed Manuel's arm again and pulled him through the door, shoving him inside the SUV as the bag of groceries in his hand clattered to the ground.

Megan fell back around the corner again, her breath

short with panic. She shielded her eyes as sand flew from the tires of the SUV and it sped back toward the highway, toward Playa Luna. She followed slowly, allowing the car to get a bit ahead of her. As it turned in to Manuel's house in the campo, she sped by, her head turned the other way. *I have to tell James,* she thought as she pushed the throttle harder, speeding up.

Running up the stairs to James's house, she heard the excited chatter of the men who had been out on the boats. As she rushed into the kitchen, she stood stock still as all the conversation stopped and all eyes were on her.

"Megan, what's the matter? What's happened? You're white as a ghost." James jumped out of his chair and rushed toward her.

Her voice caught in her throat and she grabbed the sleeve of his Hawaiian shirt, pulling him out toward the ocean. She still couldn't speak, her breaths coming in fast gulps.

James held her shoulders firmly as he searched her face. "What's happened? Calm down and breathe more slowly. You're all right."

As her nerves settled, she told him everything she had seen at the market, filling him in on the conversation she overheard. "He took Manuel, shoved him in the car and I rushed back over here."

James took in a sharp breath. "Red SUV? That's my editor, Keith."

"He was here at your house first, watching you all

through binoculars as you rounded up the smugglers. He dropped the binoculars and sped off."

He searched her face, his eyes lingering on hers for a moment.

"What possessed you to follow him? That's incredibly dangerous. What were you thinking?"

"I don't know. I...I just knew something wasn't right, and was afraid you were in danger. It was the right thing to do."

He pulled her to him, hugging her tightly.

"What are you going to do?" she asked, pulling away and looking at him quizzically. "We've got to do something for Manuel, although from the sound of it he was in on the whole thing."

As he looked out over the water, he stood for a moment as the calm sea looked blustery.

"I really didn't want to get involved. But now I have, I'll finish it up. Manuel was just trying to flesh things out. He didn't mention Keith, and headed back to the store as soon as we were finished. He did say he wanted to talk to me later."

"I want to go with you."

"No, not a chance. I don't know what this man is capable of, and I can't have you in danger. Just trust me."

With a squeeze of her hand, he rushed in the house and motioned to Kyle and Jimmy for them to follow. Fighting her instinct to tag along, she headed over to her friend's house to wait.

CHAPTER 24

Megan was flooded with relief as James, Kyle and Jimmy pulled into Felicia's driveway, seemingly all in one piece. The back-slapping and high-fives finally settled down, and they were happy to share that Keith was in police custody after what James called a "mild" altercation.

Megan pushed the button on the blender, the margarita mix and ice spinning loudly as she prepared a celebration. Pouring the icy drink into colorful glasses, she plopped a paper umbrella in each one.

"You've certainly earned this one," she said to James as she handed him a glass.

Felicia pulled the nachos she'd made out of the oven, placing them on the table between Kyle and Jimmy. "No celebration would be complete without my world-famous nachos," she laughed, sitting down beside Megan.

Kyle's mouthful of nachos didn't stop him from continuing his story. "You should have seen James when we went to Manuel's house. He was tied up to a chair. Can you believe it?"

"Seriously, I swear it was like a TV show, even watching you guys with the smugglers on the water," Felicia chimed in. "It was so exciting."

Jimmy set his glass on the table. "We really weren't sure what we were going to find, and with Manuel tied up, James just went into action."

"Oh, that's hardly what happened." James licked the salt from the side of the margarita glass, his eyes dancing with laughter. "I went over to Keith, told him to stay put, that the police were coming. He went nuts and tried to punch me. Nothing to do but hit him back."

"And lay him out flat with one punch." Kyle could hardly contain his laughter. "It was a good one," he said, grabbing for more nachos.

"What did he want with Manuel, anyway?" Megan said, still not sure what had happened.

James put his glass down and turned toward her. "After you told me about what happened at the market, and that he had taken the camera, I started thinking. Manuel had told me that Keith approached him a little while ago and offered to fund a totuaba hatchery here at the campo. Manuel agreed, but was suspicious about it. The offer kind of came out of left field, and he was concerned that Keith's stipulation was that he didn't tell me about where the funding came from."

"So he had told you about his connection with Keith, after all?" Felicia was trying to figure it all out as well.

"Yes, he did. I thought it was suspicious as well, so I didn't mention it to Keith. But when he was so adamant that I kill my smuggling story, I talked to Manuel about it again. He told me that Keith had wanted 50% of the fish that were raised for his own. When Megan told me he was so upset that we were turning in the smugglers, I realized that he must have been funding that, too. I'd planned on following up with that later, but it turned out things happened too fast."

"What? Why?" Megan exclaimed.

"I had shared my preliminary research with him awhile back. He was very interested in the price that these fish bladders are fetching if you can smuggle them over the border. Almost two million dollars for two hundred of them."

"Whoa, are you kidding? You could catch that many in a month. Did you really say two million?" Kyle asked, his eyes wide. "That's gross anyway. Who would want to pay that for a bladder?"

"It's not like a regular bladder with urine in it. It's their float bladder that fills up with gas. Keeps them buoyant. And I think that was just too much money for him to pass up. He admitted as much after he came to and we were waiting for the police. Asked me to keep it to myself, and he'd share the money with me."

Jimmy set his glass down hard. "Wait a minute. Where was I for that offer?"

He smiled around the table, and he mocked a painful grimace as Megan kicked him under the table.

"What did he want with the camera?"

"I hadn't noticed when I sent them, but it turns out that he was down here and on the boat the day I took the pictures. It was the only real evidence against him, and he wanted to make sure the police didn't get them."

"He was in the pictures? With the smugglers?" Felicia said.

James cleared his throat. "Yes, and they're in the hands of the police now. He's done for."

"Well, it was all exciting. Never had so much fun in my life," Kyle said as he stood up from the table. "So much excitement, I need to go take a nap."

Felicia laughed and stood up, clearing the dishes from the table. "Absolutely. I'll head home with you, my brave son." She poked Kyle's arm and pulled him to leave as he groaned and rolled his eyes.

"I'm out of here, too. Nicely done, James." Whiskers hopped up to follow Jimmy as he closed the door with a nod of his head to James.

James reached for Megan's hand and pulled her out onto the patio. They sat in silence briefly before he spoke.

"I can't thank you enough for following Keith. I had no idea what was going on at that point. The data card was gone, but I had another one and when I saw Keith in those pictures, I knew we were in trouble. You were really brave. I'm really proud of you."

Megan had never heard herself described as "brave" before, and it gave her shivers. Courageous in her work, maybe, but never brave. But as she thought about it, she had been brave before. Brave to open the girl's home, brave to help them at all costs, brave to take a risk. And what she'd done today was just one step further, trying to help in any way she could. She'd stepped up to the task when she needed to, and finally realized that's what she'd always done.

"I'm proud of me, too," she said as she squeezed his hand. "And I'm very relieved that everything came out all right. I was very worried when you were gone. It was all I could do not to follow."

"I'm actually surprised you didn't, but glad. I had no way of knowing what would happen, and I would have worried more if you'd been there."

And Megan had been equally worried. It had surprised her, even, that beyond just worrying about him in general, as she worried about Kyle, she'd worried even more about James. Somewhere along the line, she'd become very attached, and wanted the best for him. And for her.

He stood and pulled her up beside him.

"Well, everything's right as rain now. And going to be even better. I can tell."

He lifted her chin and placed his warm lips on hers. Her eyes fell closed and she was lost in the moment— one of the best moments she could remember. And yes, she agreed, it would only get better.

CHAPTER 25

*T*he next weeks seemed to Megan to both meander and fly by at the same time. Annie and Daniel had insisted she stay through, taking care of the potential sale and sorry they couldn't be at Cassie's wedding.

"Take lots of pictures," Annie had said. "And give them our best. We'll celebrate later."

James and Megan had fallen into a rhythm of meeting to watch the sunrise, and he continued to tell everyone around that she made better tea than anyone he'd met from across the pond. It made her smile every time he said it, and making it for him had become one of the things that made her most happy.

The afternoon before the wedding—which Megan had had no part in planning, although Cassie had come by almost daily to ask her opinion—Felicia and Megan sat under an umbrella on the beach. Felicia had her sunflower seeds and tea, and Megan had her kindle. They'd done this almost every day, between digging for clams and playing Scrabble at night with James and Kyle. The only productive thing they'd done was to put in the sink at Felicia's house, and they'd managed to do it themselves without breaking it.

"You sure you don't want some help?" James had asked as Kyle shrugged and reached for his fishing pole.

"Nope. We can do it," Megan had said, and James kissed her on the cheek before he set out behind Kyle, his own fishing pole over his shoulder.

Felicia and Megan had gone on long walks every day, talking about what Megan might do now that she wouldn't be tied to the girls' home. She still didn't know, and was sure that she would know when the time was right. They'd just been excited about the wedding, and sinking into relaxing and the rhythm of the waves, both of which were foreign to her. But she was getting the hang of it.

Megan and Felicia laughed as James held up a big fish he'd just hauled out of the surf. He looked like a kid at a candy store, and Megan loved that he was so happy. And that she was, too.

"He sure loves to fish," Felicia said. "So does Kyle, so it's been nice they can go entertain themselves."

They looked north as a Jeep pulled up, stopping right at their umbrella. Taylor and Cassie jumped out, their beach bags on their arms.

Megan hugged them both as did Felicia. The girls' tittered with excitement, and Megan was glad to see Cassie was finally getting into the spirit. Getting married was a very special occasion and she'd worried Cassie had treated it like a business event, but now she could tell that her daughter was as excited as Megan had been on her own wedding day. And that made her heart sing.

"We'll see you at five," she hollered to James. He was going to pick them up later and drive them up to Cassie's house, the Baja version of a beach carriage. The four ladies had planned to get ready at Megan's house—Cassie hadn't wanted to see Alex on the day of the wedding—and all the dresses were already there. They'd gone to town one day and scoured the shops, ending up with very colorful, Mexican style skirts for all of them but Cassie. They'd actually found a beautiful white dress that fit her perfectly and Megan had even teared up when she tried it on.

They drank a little champagne after they'd showered, and Taylor did her thing with hair and a very little bit of makeup. By the time five o'clock rolled around, they were more than ready to go.

Cassie twisted a blonde curl with her finger as she looked in the mirror, and Megan stood behind her, her hands on Cassie's shoulders. She looked around the beautiful brick bedroom, and into the mirror framed in seashells she and Cassie had found over the years.

"Did you ever think, for one second, we'd be here in

Baja getting ready for your wedding to a billionaire?" Megan tried her best not to laugh, but Cassie was having the same problem.

"No, never. Or that the sanctuary would be a reality, and we'd be building a resort?"

Megan shook her head. "No, never."

Cassie stood and turned around, wrapping her arms around her mother. "Mom, I'm so happy I could just pop."

"I'm just as happy for you, Cassie. Every mother's dream, to see her daughter so happy."

Cassie stepped back, her hands on her mother's shoulders and looked intently into her eyes. "And I want the same for you. I want you to be this happy."

"Thank you, sweetheart," Megan said as she kissed her daughter on the cheek.

"'Ello, ladies. We ready to go?" James said from the screen door. He stepped inside and stopped in his tracks. "Well, I don't believe I've seen four lovelier creatures in one place ever in my lifetime."

They all laughed and gathered their things to head to the wedding. Megan had a hard time drawing her eyes away from James, as she could say the same about him. She didn't think she'd ever met someone so kind, interesting, encouraging—and handsome. His sky blue linen shirt with white embroidery down the front was very Mexican in style, but it highlighted his eyes and they seemed to sparkle more than usual.

He escorted them all to the Range Rover, helping

each one in and making sure that no skirts got caught in car doors, and they all seemed to be overtaken by a case of nerves as they rode up the beach in silence.

They walked into the foyer and got in line, Felicia first and Taylor as the maid of honor second.

Cassie turned to Megan and said, "I am so grateful you're here to walk me down the aisle, Mom. I wouldn't want it any other way. We've made it this far on our own, and I'm honored to be walking with you now."

"Oh, don't start. I can't start crying now," Megan said as she hugged Cassie. "I'll never stop."

The music started, and as Megan walked her daughter up the aisle for what should be the happiest day of Cassie's life so far, her eyes met James's. And she realized that it was her own happiest day, too, for more reasons than one.

CHAPTER 26

*J*ames and Megan sat quietly next to each other on the cliff as the sunrise over the mountains turned the clouds orange and the water turned purple. They'd danced into the wee hours the night before at the wedding, and she wasn't sure James would be up for tea, but as it was her last day in Baja and she, Felicie and Kyle would be leaving soon, she certainly hoped he would be.

Megan laid her head gently on his shoulder as the events of the past few weeks danced slowly in her mind. So much had changed. She had changed.

"The sky is almost the colors of your scary outfit." He squeezed her hand and put his arm around her, pulling her closer.

She laughed and punched him lightly on the shoulder. "Oh, you're funny."

"Hey, I like a girl who can take risks, even if they are fashion risks."

"Not long ago, my options seemed pretty slim," she said softly. "Maybe you've convinced me that taking risks doesn't need to be scary and can still work out. It can lead to even bigger rewards."

"Do you really think you can take that chance? Make the decision to close the business and be down here? With me?"

She'd been thinking long and hard about what she was going to do—sell the business or keep trying. On the surface, the decision seemed a simple financial one, but she had gone into it with her heart wide open, hoping to help. If she left, would the girls be cared for? Would she still find ways to help? She'd spent her time in Baja trying to figure out what the next step for her should be. And whatever happened, it would have to be with the wholehearted agreement with all three part-ners—both Annie and her husband had to be on board. And from what they'd discussed over the phone, they were. Annie had explained that the company wanting to buy them out had a stellar reputation and much greater financial reserves. They could leave with full hearts, knowing that they'd done their best and that a lot of good had come of the venture.

Things had come together when Cassie and Alex had discussed options at the resort—maybe organizing some youth activities or instruction. She hadn't wanted to let James know yet about the final offer on the company, the money that would bring and the opportunity to release her from her business, to let someone else care for the girls at the ranch. But she'd made her decision, so now was the time.

"When I got here, that wouldn't have been an option. I was tied to the group home. But now that we've gotten an offer to sell it, and I actually could come down here, figure out what to do, things are different." Her eyes misted at the thought. "I never would have thought that I could be this lucky. To meet you, and have an opportunity like this. Cassie wants me at the resort and she and Alex have all kinds of ideas that sound fun. They would all make me very happy." She brushed away a tear that had trickled down her cheek.

He turned to her slowly and looked deeply into her eyes.

As he did, she felt he had shown him parts of herself that she hadn't known existed. Had opened a new world to her, both inside and out.

"Megan, would you stay here? Be with me? Travel? Be an adventurer?" he teased. "It would be a great opportunity for you to find out who you really are."

The squeaks of a baby osprey interrupted her thoughts, and they smiled, watching in silence as it followed its mother for its daily flight lesson. As she watched the birds disappear down the coast, she realized that the old, familiar knot of anxiety was gone. She felt peaceful. Content. Happy. She realized that life was still an adventure, with much more she needed to explore. And she couldn't think of anywhere she'd rather do it—or anyone she'd rather do it with.

She smiled and reached up, her lips meeting his. He wrapped his arms around her, pulling her toward him. She pulled away and let her head fall on his shoulder as she gazed out at the waves. So much had changed. She felt almost like a different person—lighter. Happier.

"Yes. I would like that. Very much. And you can call me Meg if you want to."

James let out a laugh and his eyes twinkled. "No, not now. You're Megan—a bright, shiny new Megan, and I love this one."

EPILOGUE

*M*egan packed the last of her things, and did her best not to tear up as she said goodbye to Annie and Daniel. She'd lived on the same property with her sister and brother-in-law for so long that their distance would leave a big hole in her heart. They'd all become incredibly close as they'd given their all for the girl's home, and she knew it was going to be difficult to leave after all their time together.

She and James had driven up to finalize the sale of the business, and had spent over a week packing up all of her things to take back down to the brick house in Baja. Megan carefully avoided meeting her sister's eyes, as the pained look her sister wore matched how she felt as well. She knew she'd cry when they finally had to part.

Daniel slapped James on the back as they tied the

last rope onto the truck that now held all of her belongings. The trip to Arizona had been a bittersweet one, and she took a last look at the ranch as they got ready to head back to Baja.

"Who knew you'd fall in love, we'd sell the ranch and you'd get to live full time on the beach? Lucky you," Annie said, hugging Megan tightly.

"I never thought I'd fall in love, either, but this is really the end of an era. I'm having a hard time leaving you guys."

Tears pricked her eyes as Megan hugged her sister back, not wanting to let go. She pulled away and held her sister's eyes. "I know you want to spend time with your grandkids, but please promise you'll visit as soon as you can."

Annie smiled and wiped away a tear of her own. "Just try to keep us away. The quads will stay on the trailer and we'll be down every chance we get."

"Hey, you two. We've got to get going," James said gently. "It's been wonderful to stay with you. I can see why Megan loves you so much."

"Hey, it's my turn for a hug." Daniel wrapped Megan in a bear hug.

"We couldn't have packed all of this up without you." James took one last trip around the truck, making sure everything was secured down for the long trip ahead.

As he rounded the last corner, Annie walked over to James. "I wanted to thank you, James."

"For what?" He stopped in front of her, watching her face intently as a tear left her eye and rolled down her cheek.

"The three of us have been through a lot together with the ranch. We weren't sure how it would turn out, and I've been worried about Megan. Now, with all the girls safe and sound and the business sold, I just wanted to thank you for helping her. I've never seen her this happy."

"It's been my honor," James replied with a slight bow toward Annie. "I never thought I'd fall in love, either. Your sister is the best thing that's ever happened to me. She's set me straight about how the world's supposed to be."

"Megan's good at that," Annie said with a laugh. She turned to look at Megan as she got in the truck. "I'm going to miss you."

Megan's eyes misted as she thought of the time they'd spent together, the girls they'd helped, and all the good they'd done.

"We did what we set out to do, sister. We helped a lot of kids, and that's something we can be proud of."

Annie grabbed her for one last hug. "Yes, we did do a good job, and it's all ended up for the best. It's wonderful to know you'll be happy."

Megan smiled, giving her sister a last squeeze and waving at Daniel. "And you, too, sweet sister." She turned around and looked one last time at the house, the stables and the land that had helped so many young girls. "We did good work here," she said before she got in the truck and she and James drove away.

As they drove down the road toward Mexico, Megan looked at James.

He looked in her direction. "What?"

"I heard you tell Annie that you love me," she said quietly.

He nodded. "And I heard you say the same. Funny we've never said it to each other. Isn't it about time?"

"I think we just did," Megan said with a laugh. "But for the record, I love you, James. And I've never been happier."

"Neither have I, Megan. And I love you, too."

Her small twinge of apprehension quickly subsided, and she sank into the seat, eager to get home.

Yes, happy. Finally, she thought, turning toward the road ahead.

THE END

I HOPE YOU ENJOYED As BRIGHT AS THE STARS!

Next in this series:

By The Light Of The Moon

I'd also like to introduce you to the first book in my new women's fiction series:

Newport Harbor House

If you'd like to receive an email about my new releases,
please join my mailing list.

ABOUT THE AUTHOR

Cindy Nichols writes heartwarming stories interwoven with the bonds of friendship and family that combine what she loves most about women's fiction and romance.

Cindy lives in and loves everything about the southwest, from its deserts and mountains to the sea. She discovered her passion for writing after a twenty-year career in education. When she's not writing, she travels as much as she can with her children who, although adults, still need her no matter what they think.

Feel free to sign up for her list to hear about new releases as soon as they are available. Click here to sign up: Cindy's Email List